Karri Kailamäki

Heir of the Cursed King

Karri Kailamäki

Heir of the Cursed King

Four fearsome tyrants, seven brave souls, three different worlds, one common destiny

JustFiction Edition

Impressum/Imprint (nur für Deutschland/only for Germany)
Bibliografische Information der Deutschen Nationalbibliothek: Die Deutsche Nationalbibliothek verzeichnet diese Publikation in der Deutschen Nationalbibliografie; detaillierte bibliografische Daten sind im Internet über http://dnb.d-nb.de abrufbar.
Alle in diesem Buch genannten Marken und Produktnamen unterliegen warenzeichen-, marken- oder patentrechtlichem Schutz bzw. sind Warenzeichen oder eingetragene Warenzeichen der jeweiligen Inhaber. Die Wiedergabe von Marken, Produktnamen, Gebrauchsnamen, Handelsnamen, Warenbezeichnungen u.s.w. in diesem Werk berechtigt auch ohne besondere Kennzeichnung nicht zu der Annahme, dass solche Namen im Sinne der Warenzeichen- und Markenschutzgesetzgebung als frei zu betrachten wären und daher von jedermann benutzt werden dürften.

Coverbild: www.ingimage.com

Verlag: JustFiction! Edition ist ein Imprint der
LAP LAMBERT Academic Publishing GmbH & Co. KG
Heinrich-Böcking-Str. 6-8, 66121 Saarbrücken, Deutschland
Telefon +49 681 37 20 310, Telefax +49 681 37 20 310-9
Email: info@justfiction-edition.com

Herstellung in Deutschland:
Schaltungsdienst Lange o.H.G., Berlin
Books on Demand GmbH, Norderstedt
Reha GmbH, Saarbrücken
Amazon Distribution GmbH, Leipzig
ISBN: 978-3-8454-4530-4

Imprint (only for USA, GB)
Bibliographic information published by the Deutsche Nationalbibliothek: The Deutsche Nationalbibliothek lists this publication in the Deutsche Nationalbibliografie; detailed bibliographic data are available in the Internet at http://dnb.d-nb.de.
Any brand names and product names mentioned in this book are subject to trademark, brand or patent protection and are trademarks or registered trademarks of their respective holders. The use of brand names, product names, common names, trade names, product descriptions etc. even without a particular marking in this works is in no way to be construed to mean that such names may be regarded as unrestricted in respect of trademark and brand protection legislation and could thus be used by anyone.

Cover image: www.ingimage.com

Publisher: JustFiction! Edition
is an imprint of the publishing house
LAP LAMBERT Academic Publishing GmbH & Co. KG
Heinrich-Böcking-Str. 6-8, 66121 Saarbrücken, Germany
Phone +49 681 37 20 310, Fax +49 681 37 20 310-9
Email: info@justfiction-edition.com

Printed in the U.S.A.
Printed in the U.K. by (see last page)
ISBN: 978-3-8454-4530-4

Table of Contents

Chapter I: Intro- Chaos on Earth

Long ago, when magic still existed in the world, everyone held an "Order". It was believed that Orders were something spiritual that all people got to hear once in a lifetime, and that if everyone followed their Orders it would lead the mankind to their common Destiny. It was believed that that Destiny would be to live in a paradise until the end of time.

There were three big islands that were the three kingdoms on Earth. Each of the three islands had a king who had power over smaller islands in their kingdom. One of these kings was King Henrie, the ruler over Dalik Islands. The two other kings were rulers of Mos Islands and Snow Town, the two other kingdoms.

In the beginning there was just one united nation on Earth, but because of geographical differences and groups with conversing beliefs, the humans split into three ethnic groups. Two of them were very advanced technologically, and wanted to go explore the universe on their starships, but since it was against the ancient religion of the third group of humans, they were only ones that stayed on the planet. They soon took control of all the land that their former neighbors had left behind. Since the Earth was too big for one person to rule, and there were still groups with different beliefs the borders of the three kingdoms remained, and two new rulers were voted to reign over Mos Islands and the enormous Snow Town.

There were not any wars or hatred. Everyone lived in peaceful harmony; men, dragons, wolves, and all other creatures on the planet accepted each other as they were. When the three kings were all in their thrones, it opened a magical path to the Middle Island, which was the island that was shared by everyone. Anyone from any kingdom could come there. The Middle Island was loved by everyone.

Life was happy until the day that changed everything. All of a sudden, a flagitious sorcerer called Raiwox took over the Middle Island with his followers, and incarcerated the three kings to the Underworld. The gate to the Middle Island was now closed, and Raiwox built a castle there and crowned himself as the one and only King of the World. No one could have stopped his abrupt rise to power. No one even knew where he had gained such might to be able to overthrow the three rightful kings.

Now that Raiwox was the ruler, Earth was in total chaos: people fought for the three kingdoms, because the one who touched the throne became the new king according to the Book of Magical Order. Old good kings were soon replaced with new, evil ones. Innocents were eliminated by the greedy and selfish megalomaniacs who craved for power. For them, control over others was more important than everyone getting along. The path to Middle Island remained shut, because only the presence of the original kings on their thrones could keep the path open.

The four tyrants sent atrocious creatures called 'Tax Ghosts', cloaked figures with scythes, to collect unfairly high taxes from the people. They were zombies that walked from door to door and eliminated anyone who refused, or could not pay. These monsters were as much feared as

Raiwox' underlings that wrecked havoc, destroying cities where resistance groups existed and killing or enslaving all who dared to even plan opposition to the New World.

Raiwox was in charge of the evil kings and the entire Earth. He sent his armies of Kuoles, creatures of the underworld, to terminate the uprisings all over the world. Gates to the underworld were open in random places, and awakened demons took over bodies of pilgrimages, which did not bother the merciless rulers as it only granted them more mindless servants. The self-proclaimed King of the World offered dark powers and authority to those who agreed to side with him. This attracted some people who had once been good to serve the conqueror. On the other hand, some rebels were killed publicly in such brutal ways that it scared many citizens to just accept Raiwox's order.

All the confusing events that had suddenly changed the way of life on Earth had happened very fast. Almost no one who opposed any of the new kings, survived. Some people who were against the new order tried to bring back the original kings from the Underworld to restore the peace, but no one ever succeeded. These brave souls that did not support Raiwox were called The Last Warriors of Light. One of them, a young man named Akii, tried to set his king, King Henrie of Dalik Islands, free, but got trapped in the Underworld himself like many other warriors before him. This courageous young man heard his Order that day, and the holy voice told him to choose his most trustworthy friend to bring back the peace and freedom.

So, with his last ounce of power, Akii sent a magical letter from the depths of the horrific Underworld to his best friend, Salosti. He had no idea where Salosti could be or was he even alive after all the spreading madness had born, but Salosti was the only hope.

End of the Chapter I

Chapter II: The Last Warriors of Light

Far away from everything, in the middle of an otherwise empty field, there was a tower. It was an enormous edifice that could be spotted from far away. No one ever dared to enter it, since rumors said that a grumpy sorcerer lived there. People who possessed strong magical powers were greatly feared in those times. In fact, there were only few that even had the courage to come out of their homes anymore ever since Raiwox took control of the planet, and the few that did were cautious like hunted game.

The wizard in the tower had not been heard of since the madness had begun in the kingdom. Some said he was dead. Others suspected something else. In any case, no one ever saw him again. The nightmare had begun long ago...

Salosti was wandering alone in a green forest. His home had been attacked by the Kuoles, but he had managed to escape. Traumatized by the sight of death and destruction, he did not have the least idea what he was supposed to do now. He didn't know what was happening, why the sky had suddenly turned blood red, and why there were dark creatures running wildly, demolishing everything on their path. He needed an explanation, but did not know where to go or who to turn to. There was no one around in the emerald woods; not even the small, luminous fairies that usually lighted the darkness for travelers. Everywhere was quiet and empty. All of a sudden the lively and sunny lands had turned dark and deserted. There was no other choice but to run and hide in hopes of not getting caught by the monsters that had unexplainably appeared.

Suddenly Salosti saw something shiny floating towards him. It was too big to be a fairy. Our hero stopped and looked closely at it. It was a magical letter. Salosti grabbed the letter and it stopped shining. He had heard that only wizards of great magical powers could send these kinds of letters. He read it slowly with excitement.

Dear, Salosti

It is a joyous miracle itself if this letter has reached you, but this is not the time to rejoice. Please prepare yourself emotionally, for what you are about to read may very well overwhelm you.

There is no way on Earth you haven't noticed all this chaos spreading like a wildfire, but the cause may be a mystery to you. If it has not yet been brought to your knowledge, a powerful black sorcerer called Raiwox has trapped not only our king, Henrie, but all the other kings as well into the Underworld. He is behind all the changes; the Tax Ghosts, the tyrant kings, the monsters. I tried to save our king, but failed and got trapped here myself. I was too reckless and underestimated the enemy, and now I'm paying the price in this infernal prison.

Right the moment I was captured by the monsters I heard my Order. To explain the feeling in words is simply impossible; it was like God Himself spoke to me. According to the holy voice I am to choose the most trustworthy person I know. The first person that came to mind was you, and there was no one else who I'd think would be brave or dumb enough to help. Thus I chose you, my best friend, to save us and the whole earth.

I know it sounds impossible, but God has given me his word, and by following His will we will all be fine in the end. Here is your mission:

You must destroy the evil kings that have taken over the three thrones. Also, you must rescue me and the three original kings from the Underworld.

When the original kings have been returned to their thrones, it'll allow us to go to the Middle Island where Raiwox has built his Citadel of Darkness. Together we shall defeat him.

But since you are not a skilled warrior, nor a wizard, it is impossible for you to do this all without help. Therefore, you need to find good, trustworthy people who will follow you as The Last Warriors of Light. These people will become your army and will help you on your quest.

Be wary of demons and Kuoles on your way. They attack when you least expect it. Also, you must always carry some money with you so you won't be killed in you run into a Tax Ghost.

This is all very much asked, but I know you can do it. I trust you.

- Akii

Salosti was speechless. *He* would have to save the world! He, who was merely an orphan farmer who had escaped from his adoptive parents few months ago. He, who had been seen as a wretched child and a delinquent for his rebellious attitude. It all seemed so wrong. It must've been a misunderstanding. But Salosti knew the time was running out, so he had to get an army and quickly. He recalled his mission, and read the letter one last time. He even pinched himself to see if it was a dream. It was not.

The confused teenager walked along a long and dusty road. He hid every time he heard voices. They were definitely either Kuoles or demons. He wished he had a sword or magical powers to protect himself. Unfortunately he was just a poor flaneur who had gotten separated from all his friends of his hometown. Well, truthfully Dalik City was not where he had born; his real hometown was a small hamlet a few kilometers away, but since he had escaped in search of adventures at age eleven, and had found friends in the capital of the kingdom, he had decided to stay there.

At any rate, he needed to find someone who could forge him a sword, and someone who could teach him magic. He knew Akii to be a skilled Royal Guard, and even he had been captured by the dark creatures.

After a while Salosti came to an intersection. He read a sign that said: Unhorimes.

"Unhorimes, huh?" Salosti thought aloud. "I hope I can find there some people that'll believe me and join my army."

Meanwhile in the underworld Akii and King Henrie began to fall into state of desperation. It had been days since the letter had been sent, and in the infernal darkness it felt even longer.

"Sir, do you think my letter reached Salosti?" Akii asked hopefully from his master.

"It probably did, but it'll take him ages to gather up an army and find the portal here. I'm afraid that we must stay here still a little longer, my friend," King Henrie replied gloomily. The Underworld was a horrible place. All one could see was infinite darkness. Voices of pain echoed in nothingness and Kuoles crowded the places.

Akii looked up and saw the above world with the eyes of his soul. Oh, how he wished he would be freed, so that he could fight alongside his friend and restore the blackened kingdoms to their former glory.

"Your majesty, do you believe in the Orders? Did I do the right thing when I chose Salosti? Is everything going to be okay?"

The king looked at him sadly: "The Orders are true for sure, but I can't tell if they lead us to a happy ending. We just need to pray and wish everything will be fine."

Salosti wandered aimlessly in the town, trying to find a way to the dark castle that was standing on the highest hill. One of the three tyrants was there. Salosti knew it, because he had heard copious rumors about a callous ruler in the town of Unhorimes. The town was filled with inns and hotels and other abandoned buildings. No person was outside. Salosti wasn't even sure if there were any people left in the whole town.

It may very well be possible they're all dead or enslaved. I've even heard that they can turn humans into Tax Ghosts and Kuoles.

Abruptly Salosti turned around as he heard someone running from behind him yelling:

"Salosti, wait!" The boy turned around and saw Hajosiko, Liisa and Kaste, his old friends from Dalik Islands. Salosti had not seen his childhood friends for months, so he was obviously relieved that they were okay. He used to play with the three and Akii in Dalik Islands, and they had always had very much fun.

"Hey, guys! I'm so happy to see you all okay!" Salosti exclaimed joyfully. It felt almost unreal to see all his friends unharmed after all that had taken place. "Where have you been?"

"We were captured and sent into a horrible place called Child Center," Liisa explained, "It's a place where Raiwox sends children to be manipulated, so they would accept his totalitarian authority. We've never been mistreated that badly. But thanks to a certain person we escaped. We immediately started searching for you, but never did we expect it to be this easy. You were in the very same town!"

"Thank goodness that we found each other," Hajosiko said relieved.

"But you cannot come with me!" Salosti said, looking down. He had been so scared for his three friends, but now that he knew they were fine he wanted them to find a safe place to stay, so he would have a place to return to after his quest. "I am going to defeat the evil kings and Raiwox..."

"So are we," Hajosiko said. He was Salosti's second best friend next to Akii, even though he had always been sort of a rival to him. Hajosiko liked to tease his friends and was usually very carefree.

 "None of you is skilled enough to defeat them all alone" Salosti said, protesting the idea of the three joining forces with him, although the courageous offer did make him feel supported. "Go find a place where the monsters won't find you. I need to raise an army to defeat the evil king who rules this town. It was Akii's Order to make me take the quest to return the peace, so I must do it. Otherwise it'd be going against the will of our God. Furthermore, no human can enjoy living under these conditions. Even the ones who have defected to Raiwox's side did so only out of fear. This world needs to be saved."

"We'll be your army!" Liisa said without hesitation. She was a beautiful and smart girl with a straight brown hair and a white dress. Though Salosti never admitted it, he had a crush on her.

"What? I can't approve of that!" Salosti said. "You and Kaste are girls. I cannot let you two get in danger for me."

"Of course we'll help you; you're our friend," Kaste winked. She had a blonde hair, and she was Liisa's best friend. She was the leader type person. "We're coming along whether you want it or not."

"Fine," Salosti acquiesced. He knew there was nothing he could say to make Liisa or Kaste change their minds. They were too stubborn and caring to allow their friend go by himself.

"But we are going to need more people for our army. Then we must buy some weapons, equipment and perhaps magic. Once we've trained our skills we are ready to face the evil kings and then Raiwox himself."

Salosti sighed as recalling the mission somehow made it sound that much harder; it would take them ages. Furthermore, just four people wasn't much of an army. There were four tyrants in total, all of whom had armies of their own. Nonetheless, our hero was relieved to see his friends again. And at the very least he had found people who were definitely trustworthy. He would trust his life in the hands of his friends. They had been through a lot of things that had strengthened their bonds.

"Where do we find more people for our army?" Salosti wondered aloud. "Four warriors is certainly a little too few to be called and army. That, and none of us is capable of fighting the monsters."

"We've heard that no one on Earth is good anymore, so we're just gonna find some people that aren't from Earth," said Liisa as if it wasn't a big deal leaving the planet.

"What! How's that possible?" Salosti asked perplexed.

Liisa explained:

"We found a Falgomduzian space ship in a hiding place where we ran after the attack of the Kuoles. We stayed there until the coast was clear. Then we went to look for you."

Falgomduzians were one of the two groups of technologically advanced humans who left the planet centuries ago. History books were filled with information about them, but nobody knew where exactly they lived in the galaxy currently.

"Okay, now since everything's solved, shall we go to our space ship?" Hajosiko said and showed the way to the hiding place. On the way, Salosti explained all about his mission given to him by Akii who had heard his Order in the underworld.

Soon the four reached the hiding place where the space ship was. They had gotten there without running into any Kuoles or Tax Ghosts. Salosti was amazed to see the ship: it was even more beautiful than he had imagined. The current Earth's people had only steam engines, so he had never seen or expected something with as complicated structure and vast list of functions.

"This thing's amazing!" he praised, admiring the beautifully shaped, silver-colored ship from each angle.

"Don't say anything before we've blasted off," Hajosiko said proudly as if he had built it.

Soon all the four were sitting inside the space ship. Luckily there was enough space for everyone. Liisa said that they had tested the ship before and it worked. Also there was a storage full of fuel, so they wouldn't have to worry about running out of it.

"Are you sure there is any intelligent life out there?" Salosti asked. Nothing had been heard of the two other groups of humans ever since they had left the planet.

"There must be! It's our only hope. Otherwise we'll have to fight by ourselves."

"We'll just hope we find either the Falgomduzians or WOPlings," Liisa said, "But then there's the question how we get them to come and help us."

"We'll think about that later. Now let's go!" Kaste said.

The countdown started. "Three, two, one, BLAST OFF!"

The ship launched with extreme speed. Salosti was flattened against his seat and was happy that he hadn't eaten for a while. The speed was so incredible that he thought that his eyes were going to fall off. For the first hundred meters he felt sick and insecure in the strong vibration of his seat. He couldn't hear anything but the thunder of the engine. He tried to turn his head to see how the others were doing, but couldn't because of the pressure.

Soon the ship became stable and floated smoothly as if it was in water. Someone shouted: "Look!" Salosti could now turn his head and he looked out of the window to see an infinite ocean of stars. Never before had he seen anything that beautiful. He felt free now more than ever and he was happy. The only thing that almost matched this feeling was when he escaped from his old home and became independent and free.

"Wow! What a great view," Hajosiko yelled over Liisa's head.

The trip took many hours. Salosti kept expressing his gratitude to God for finding his friends. That was when Liisa revealed something strange:

"It's kind of embarrassing," she said, "but I could somehow feel your presence in Unhorimes. I don't know how, but I'm sure that is how we found you."

 After three hours everybody was sleeping except Hajosiko, since he was the one controlling the ship. Having read the manual many times, it was rather easy, and most of the functions were automatic. The boy wondered if the ship was a spare one of if the people who had built it had intentionally left it there for somebody to find. The idea to go and find someone from another planet had come from a shy little girl in the Child Center when all the young prisoners there were planning an escape.

"Perhaps she heard her Order," Hajosiko thought, "Because I would never have thought of that. If we really do find some help it must really be true that the Orders control our Destiny."

Finally, after traveling hundreds of light years, the space ship landed smoothly on an unknown surface. The Warriors were in a planet called Falgomduza, though they didn't know it. It was the very place that the group of former Earthlings had made their new home. Everybody came out of the ship and looked around. The planet had more wild nature than Earth. There were brown hills and black, snowy mountains in the distance. As for buildings, only a few cottages were scattered here and there. It looked rather deserted.

There were no people, but the kids knew that at least something must live there because of the cottages. Salosti saw a boy fishing on a pier. The boy wore black and white clothes and his hair was sticking out like Salosti's. Only his hair was green like seaweed.

Salosti yelled at him: "Hey there!" The boy turned around and Salosti walked by him.

"Listen up because I'm going to tell this only once: We're from planet Earth, and our world is in danger; a tyrant named Raiwox has taken over our entire planet, and is planning to expand his realms till the end of universe. Now where are all the people, especially grownups? We need help."

The boy was puzzled. He stood up and Salosti saw that they were both as tall.

"You're from another world? Please tell me, have you heard of a person named Vatarki?"

"Huh? I don't think..."

"I've heard of him! He's the tyrant king of Unhorimes" Kaste broke in. "He's one of the new, evil ones. What about him?"

The boy sighed.

"He's my brother you see. This planet used to have magical crystals created by a secret society, for each of the three nations. The three crystals were called Crystals of Falgomduza. My brother escaped from home, stole all the crystals and connected them to make their magical powers even stronger. He planned to take over this world, but I stopped his plans. I got all the crystals back and burned them. I thought they would never cause any more trouble, but I think I was wrong. Half a year ago my brother went to search for the crystal-dust that was the result of burned crystals. The dust still had the same powers as their solid form, you see? I think that if he found the crystal-dust, he'll be unstoppable. He must've found it, because now he's a tyrant king in your world."

"Yeah, but he doesn't have power over Raiwox, though; otherwise he would be the main tyrant in the Middle Island," Salosti said. "I wonder what makes Raiwox even more powerful than Vatarki with the crystal-dust. He must have discovered a source of power that is even more incredible."

The teenagers contemplated a little.

"By the way, is your name Salosti?" The boy asked out of the blue.

Salosti was amazed.

"How the heck did you know my name?"

"I heard my Order, which told me to come with you and your army. However, I was prohibited to take anybody else with me."

Salosti sighed and moaned: "So, we came all this way to get only one kid to join us."

The boy seemed embarrassed and degraded. Kaste broke in quickly.

"Don't mind Salosti. He's sometimes like that. Let's introduce ourselves. Hi, I'm Kaste."

Liisa and Hajosiko introduced themselves as well. Then the boy talked:

"Nice to meet you guys! My name's Dani. I'm joining your army and I'm ready to go whenever you want."

The five walked to the space ship and launched from the Falgomduza's surface, switching the course back to Earth. Once again they enjoyed the views. Salosti thought that the trip hadn't been futile after all. He did not admit it, though. If Dani had really heard his Order, then he could be useful. But why in the world could they not take more Falgomduzians along?

We've got to hope that there are still good people on Earth too, Salosti thought.

The army enjoyed the traveling through the space, going around the sun, but little did they know about Raiwox's surprise waiting them back on Earth.

The space ship landed smoothly on Earth's surface. Hajosiko was really good at controlling it. The five kids came out and were searching to get back their balance.

"Space is amazing!" Dani exclaimed still amazed of the beautifulness he had just seen. Everybody agreed.

Suddenly Liisa shrieked. Salosti turned around and saw some dark, shapeless creatures dashing towards the group. They were Kuoles that had waited there to ambush the group. How they had found the spot nobody knew, nor did they have time to think.

The creatures tried to grab on them and succeeded on Liisa. She screamed and Hajosiko was kicking and hitting the monsters, but they were not affected. Kaste ran away screaming. Salosti was still confused and tried to go save his friends, but Dani beckoned him to stand back.

"Lemme handle them," he said mysteriously and Salosti saw something black in the Falgomduzian boy's fist. Dani started to yell some weird words that Salosti didn't understand. As he yelled the words, something happened to the creatures: One was impaled by ice-sticks that suddenly stuck from the ground. Another was stricken by a lightning. The third-one was burned with fire.

As the creatures were wounded by the powerful spells, they disappeared, turning into a black dust that was blown out by the wind. Everything was quiet again. Salosti noticed that his mouth was wide open and he closed it quickly. Liisa, Hajosiko, and Kaste walked by Salosti and Dani.

Dani smiled at Salosti proudly, a little braggingly, but the other boy only gave him a jealous look. Liisa, Hajosiko and Kaste all were talking at the same time.

"That was amazing!"

"How'd you do that?"

"What were those things?"

Dani seemed to be happy about all the attention and admiration he had gotten, and Salosti looked at him even more jealously.

"Quiet, please," Dani said patiently like an idol and cleaned his throat, preparing for an explanation that would make him popular in this company.

"Those were Kuoles, Raiwox's minions. I heard about them in my Order. I should think that Raiwox has found out our location and sent those things after us. The way I got rid of them was magic, which I learned from my parents. I also had a teacher in my planet who used to fight in the military and taught me some self-protective spells."

He looked around and continued.

"Seems like we need to shop some weapons and spells for you guys; otherwise you wouldn't be able to protect yourselves from armies of Kuoles, which surely will be sent soon to get us, since we beat those ones with ease."

Salosti asked Dani what it was like to hear the Order, but he only gave the same vague explanation Akii had given in his letter. None of the other warriors had yet heard their Orders, so they wondered what it was like to go through that spiritual enlightenment.

The Warriors walked in the town searching for a shop in which they could buy some weapons, armors, and equipment. Luckily Dani was from a wealthy noble family, and had all his money with him. Soon the kids found a shop with an honest vendor selling the equipment. The vendor sold everything in his shop for special price, because he hadn't had customers in months. He said that everyone had disappeared from the town one by one. He suspected that they had been turned into Tax Ghosts and Kuoles.

Each warrior got armor and a helmet. Everyone could choose their weapons which would determine their 'positions' in the battle front. Those positions were invented by Salosti. He created this table to help his army choose their positions:

Positions

Sword= Attacker- fighting in the first place

Staff= Supporter- supports Attackers and Defenders by using magic

Shield or Heavy Armor= Defender- Defends Attackers and Supporters with a shield

-Salosti became an Attacker with his light sword

-Hajosiko became a Supporter with his staff and magic

- Liisa became another Attacker with her two daggers

- Kaste chose to be a Defender with her shield and spear

- Dani wanted to be one of all positions with his long sword, strong hereditary magic, and shield

---

The shopping was done soon and the vendor told the kids to be careful. Dani had spent all his money. Besides spells and weapons, he had bought a camping set, sleeping bags and back-bags for everyone to carry. Of course they also got some food.

Salosti had contradictory opinions about Dani. He didn't know yet did he like him or not. Dani seemed to be nice and a good fighter, but he also seemed to take over the control of the army, even though Salosti had made it clear that he was the leader, since he had been chosen by Akii. Also Dani seemed already more popular than Salosti, making him jealous of Dani. But he didn't know why it was so, and he refused to admit the jealousy himself.

The army was walking in the empty town. Sky was red and it was sunset. Suddenly, after being quiet for ten minutes, Salosti came up with an idea.

"I know how to get our army!" The four others turned around to look at him as he continued "Dani had the Order to join this army. So, we'll just make a notification to the people of this town to join this army in case that they've heard their Orders too. If all who God has chosen stand up against the kings of injustice together, we'll surely defeat them."

Everybody cheered and agreed. Salosti felt proud and more comfortable when he had expressed his brilliant idea. He was secretly glad that no one else had come up with it, though it would have helped greatly.

This is what was written in notifications all over the town:

Dani used his magic to send the notifications to the other two kingdoms as well. The army members knew Raiwox's servants could notice them and try and join the army to slay all of them. That was why safety precautions were made; Dani used magic to modify the notification papers so that only people who had heard their Orders could understand them.

"Having heard your Order changes the way you see things," he explained.

Salosti was leaning against the cold wall in the abandoned school that the army had chosen as its hiding place. There Dani had spent the last five hours teaching the others proper spell-casting and swordplay. In the middle of clanking swords and shiny spells Salosti was fantasying about the day he and his army would finally destroy Raiwox. He had always been looked down upon by the people of his town for the fact that he was an uncivilized orphan who always acted on his emotions. He was sure that saving the Earth would show those prejudicial fools who he really was, and make them respect him. But that was not the sole reason why he was so determined; he also wanted to end the madness and return home safely with Akii and the others. Salosti had always been defiant of authority, and thus could not stand a quartet of tyrants reigning with their unfair, selfish laws.

"Salosti!"

Salosti raised his head and saw Kaste and said: "I'm sorry, what?"

"Are you deaf or what?" she said, but not too angrily. She was actually amused. "I called you three times! Were you thinking about Liisa?"

"What? No!" Salosti denied, turning red even though he was speaking the truth. He glanced to the back of the room to see if the brunette girl had heard, but she was just practicing her spells. Noticing the boy's stare she waved at him with a smile. Salosti looked away quickly and turned back to Kaste, "At any rate, what did you want to tell me?"

"Our army's here! There are people who actually read our notification."

Salosti stood up and walked to the door. He saw four people standing outside: Two young men that looked identical (twins, maybe?), a strong looking boy with wide muscles, and an extremely small, maybe nine years old, boy wearing colorful clothes.

"You've gotta be kidding me! Four people!" Salosti said a little disappointed. "That makes only eight of us in total. Well, I guess we must go with what we have. So, who are you people?"

"I'm Lumi," said the strong looking guy. He had a long shaft in his belt in which there was a sword with a golden handle. With a first look he seemed like he would be a decent attacker. "I come from King's Valley near Snow Town. My father's a famous hunter and I've learned lots of survival skills and battle moves from him."

Salosti nodded approvingly, and moved his eyes to the next Warrior candidate to allow him to introduce himself.

"Ferry and David," said the bearded man pointing first himself and then his brother. Salosti evaluated them to be tough by their appearance. "We are Knights of the Twilight from the Sadesia Territory. We have protected our village for five years, and slain two wild dragons that threatened our peace."

"How good is your gear?" Salosti inquired. This time the other person, David, answered:

"Our mythril swords are capable of piercing through steel armors."

"Oh really?" said the impressed leader. He turned to the last person in the line; the little one.

"Eric," said the small boy. "I'm from the Sacred Mountains. I don't have any great accomplishments, but I will do anything to kill Raiwox to avenge the death of my parents."

Eric was the only one that Salosti did not see as a good addition to the army. He didn't think that the little kid was not worthy or anything, but he did not want the little one to get hurt. The battles against the tyrants were not going to be anything that such little kids could handle.

"You three are okay," Salosti said to Lumi, Ferry and David. "But what're you doing here?" he asked from Eric.

"I heard my Order, which was the only requirement, right?" said Eric, protecting his rights.

"Well, I wasn't expecting someone like you..." Salosti started, but Eric started to scream as if in panic.

"Please let me stay! I can help you; I found the portal to the Underworld!"

Salosti gasped: "YOU WHAT!"

End of Chapter II: The Last Warrior's of Light

Chapter III: Salvation

Salosti dashed towards the young Eric who was terrified about the sudden reaction. The leader of the army shook the little boy from the sleeve of his jacket yelling: "Tell me where you saw the portal to the Underworld!"

He could not help being impetuous. The place where his best friend and his king were waiting in torture was in the knowledge of that child.

"Aah! Put me down, put me down!" cried the little boy.

Salosti realized he had acted a little heavy-handed, loosed his grip and put Eric, who was still shaking and almost cried, down. Eric looked around nervously. Kaste came by him and patted his head gently like a mother comforting her child.

"Don't be shy; we won't hurt you," she said and glared angrily at Salosti, who spread his arms in "what-did-I-do?" position.

Eric spoke: "I… I saw the portal in the forest, outside the town…"

"That's where we gonna go!" Salosti interrupted and turned to face Lumi, David and Ferry

"I assume you guys are prepared for fights that may ensure." The three nodded. Ferry and David took out their green-bladed swords to show they were ready. The former claimed that their shields were fire and spell proof.

"Same here," Lumi said, "I stole all of my father's protective gear. He has survived a Killer Fox's attack with them."

 "Good," Salosti said and stood up on a platform that was used to give speeches. He faced his entire army and spoke:

"The Last Warriors of Light; I'll split you into two groups as the place is probably vast. Hajosiko and Lumi, go with Kaste and Liisa, and remember to protect the girls. This group's gonna look for enemies; if you find any, just yell. Ferry, David, and Dani are another group; warriors. You fight the enemies in the first place. I'll go alone as the seeker; I'm gonna seek for Akii and Henrie."

"Don't you think we should prepare a little better," said Dani like a know-it-all.

"We don't have time for that," Salosti said, "The portals to the Underworld only stay in one spot for a set time before they appear elsewhere. Besides, we should do just fine with the weapons and spells we have bought. Moreover, we have five destined people, and it's our mission to save King Henrie and Akii."

"Okay, now! Everything's ready, let's go!"

"Wait!" Eric was hanging in Salosti's jacket just when he was about to leave. "What about me?"

"Oh, yeah, Eric! You'll get an important part of the mission: You'll be… um… watching this secret place! Don't let anybody in! And stay here till we get back!" Salosti went outside with his army heading to the forest, and left Eric alone in the cold, empty, abandoned school.

Eric was very mad at Salosti who already treated him like a baby. He decided to exit the building and go fight Vatarki by himself. That was what he was Ordered to do, after all. He thought that if he succeeded, the people would start to respect him. So, he headed for the dark castle on the hill all alone.

Salosti and the others reached the outskirts of Emerald Forest outside the town. They spread out and started to look for a portal. The bushes and trees were thick and green. It was the most colourful place left on earth; the only place that had not been painted with gray and black.

Soon Hajosiko yelled that he had found the portal. Everybody approached and saw him pointing at a black orb-like thing. It glowed and was surrounded by dancing shadows. Salosti touched the orb and saw his hand disappear into it like it was being devoured. He drew it back quickly to see it was still in one piece. Then he talked.

"I'll go first, but if I don't return immediately, don't follow; it may be a trap." Salosti turned back to face the orb.

"Okay… on three! One, two… three…" Salosti didn't jump. He didn't move at all. "What if I'm gonna die?" he thought.

"Okay, second try: one, two… - three…" Salosti hesitated and made a sudden move forward, but drew himself quickly back. It was harder that trying to jump into ice cold water; he feared for his life.

"Think about it this way, Salosti," Hajosiko said "You're gonna do it anyway, so it really doesn't matter when you go. So, why don't you go now, try again?" Hajosiko's advice encouraged Salosti a little.

"Okay this time…" Salosti said and felt someone's hands in his back that pushed him into the dark orb.

Everybody looked at Lumi who had pushed Salosti.

"Why'd you do that?" Hajosiko said angrily.

"Well, as you said, he was gonna do it anyway. I only helped him a little," Lumi replied, acting all innocent.

"Still that wasn't necessary" Hajosiko continued. Lumi only gave him an annoying, contemptuous face. Hajosiko hated him already.

"Who wants to go next?" Kaste wondered.

Salosti fell all the way down till he hit the ground. The drop had been about one and a half meters, and Salosti had hurt his crotch. He observed his surroundings; he was in the Underworld, which seemed to be some kind of catacomb. Scary sounds echoed from afar and it was difficult to see.

Suddenly, all the other kids fell from the portal next to him landing roughly. They were groaning and Salosti was mad.

"Why did you all come at the same time? And what did I just tell you above? You were not supposed to come till I'd have given you a sign!"

Everybody pointed at Lumi and Salosti dashed towards him.

"What the hell do you think you're doing?"

"I wanted to make sure that nobody cheats. Maybe one of us could have been a traitor who would have closed the exit after the others had gotten in."

"If someone here's a traitor, that's you!"

Lumi looked at Salosti gloomily talking from between his teeth: "Don't call me a traitor. I'm not a traitor!"

Suddenly he cast an ice spell on Salosti, who raised his arm out of reaction. Salosti's arm was now covered with an ice-layer. Salosti withdrew his sword and slashed it through the air while casting a wind-spell. Lumi flew through the air and crashed on a pillar, damaging it viciously.

Ferry, Dani, David and Hajosiko rushed to calm Lumi. Soon Ferry was holding Lumi in a grip that made him unable to move. Salosti melted the ice from his arm with a mild fire-spell. The other boys were on the sides of Lumi ready to catch the young man if he happened to get free from Ferry's lock. Kaste and Liisa had concealed themselves behind a rock.

"Kill him," Ferry said, "he attacked Salosti. He must be a servant of Raiwox."

Liisa walked by Salosti.

"Salosti, we must let him stay... he had the Order..."

Salosti interrupted her.

"We have no proof that he heard the Order. We have no proof about any Orders of you guys. You may all be traitors sent by Raiwox, assigned to kill me immediately when you get the chance."

"Salosti, I swear that Hajosiko, Kaste and I are in your side. I know them, and so do you. And you know me…" She looked directly at Salosti's eyes. He felt warm inside for a moment. He tore himself from the good feeling.

"I don't know any of you guys, and I don't know can I trust you," he said and sighed. "But I guess I have no choice."

He turned back to face Lumi who had now calmed down.

"Make sure, this doesn't happen again; not between you and me, and not between anybody else."

"Yes… Salosti" he replied humbly. "I'm sorry, but what you said reminded me of a memory of my past that made me infuriated. I'll try to control myself the next time."

Ferry loosened his grip of Lumi and Salosti started giving orders.

"There're many chambers in here; I'll check this-one, and you pick another one. Keep your weapons ready and remember your duties! We'll meet at this exact place in an hour." Salosti disappeared into one of the caves.

Hajosiko, Kaste, Liisa, David, Lumi, Ferry and Dani withdrew their weapons and went another way. They found enemies immediately; they were same kind of Kuoles as on above the ground. Ferry and David fought well against the first enemy team, but they kept on coming. Dani and Hajosiko helped. Liisa and Kaste were in a trouble. Hajosiko helped them out, and reminded Lumi to fight near to the girls.

"I got work to do here; you take care of them," Lumi said indifferently.

Hajosiko wasn't the only one sick of Lumi; Dani shouted over the noises of fight: "Lumi, do as Salosti told you to do!"

Lumi moaned annoyingly and obeyed.

Salosti was confused with the directions in the catacomb since every place looked the same. "Did I just come from here? Is this a new place?"

The Underworld was like a labyrinth. Some caves had a dead end, and the other's led him deeper to the maze.

Our hero went on fighting the enemies on the way. The Kuole troops seemed endless, and although they were rather easy to defeat with his expensive gear, they sure slowed him down.

Finally he found a chamber bigger than others. He couldn't get inside, because there was some kind of invisible wall blocking the entrance. Salosti tried his sword and all the spells he knew. It was pretty beautiful to see how the spells were cast and stopped in the air and mixed up. The mixture of colors in the invisible wall started to glow and then exploded.

Salosti could now get through, and so he did. There were no enemies in the big chamber, like there were in anywhere else. Salosti saw a huge castle that looked more like a rock. Two people were coming down the stairs of the castle's entrance and Salosti recognized the figures immediately: His best friend, Akii and his majesty, King Henrie. The two saw Salosti and came running by him.

"Thank you, Salosti! I can't tell how happy I'm to see you. I knew you would come!" Akii said. King Henrie came to shake Salosti's hand. He was crying and Salosti was surprised to see how sentimental he was.

"Thank you, son! May Gods bless you!"

Salosti tried to tear himself out of the good feeling, because he knew that the mission was still unaccomplished.

"Hey, guys. I know you're excited to get free and you've been waiting for this for a long time, but we really need to get outta here and quickly. This place's crawling with enemies!"

"Speak of the devil!" Henrie yelled while pointing upwards: a whole army of Kuoles was dashing towards the four from above.

"Great!" Salosti said vexed. "You two, go to the above-world with my army. Just follow the noises of fighting and you'll find them. I'll slow down these guys, and come afterwards!"

Akii and Henrie started running and Salosti withdrew his sword and charged an attack on the nearest ten Kuoles. They were taken down easily. Salosti spun with his sword and got rid of Kuoles that surrounded him. The dark monsters started to get angrier and attacked Salosti with more confidence. The warrior got many scratches. He slashed with his sword and cast spells on the enemies that seemed even more endless. Finally he decided to flee. There was no way he could keep up with the numbers.

Hajosiko, Lumi, Dani, Ferry, David, Liisa and Kaste were still fighting at the same spot. Then Dani recognized the duo in the distance.

"Look, it's King Henrie and that friend of the Leader."

"So all we need to do now is to get outta here," Kaste said.

"Wait!" Liisa yelled. "What about Salosti?"

"He said that he'll come after us," Akii explained while running.

The ten went to the portal.

Soon, Dani, Liisa, Kaste, Ferry, Lumi, David, Henrie, Hajosiko and Akii found themselves back in the forest outside Unhorimes. They were all exhausted, but could now sigh out of relief they had survived.

"Sunlight is so bright!" Henrie said whining and covering his face with his hands. His eyes had accustomed to the darkness of the Underworld.

"What are you? A vampire?" Hajosiko joked around. Akii was shocked.

"How are you addressing his highness? You should call him "your majesty" or at least "sir"!"

Hajosiko was embarrassed by his own indecency.

"I'm sorry, I was just joking around. I didn't know he was…"

King Henrie broke in.

"No need to worry! I no longer care about noble treatment. You can just call me Henrie."

"But Mr. the King Sir, shouldn't you be little more dignified?" Akii said.

"Bah, I lost my power and dignity when I lost my throne. Now I'm just like you people."

Then Akii remembered that Salosti who was still in the Underworld.

"What's taking him so long?"

Just when he said that, Salosti came from the portal. He was panting and full of scratches. Hajosiko came by him and healed his wounds with a spell. He sure deserved his position as the main supporter, because his aiding spells were very effective.

"Those (huff, huff)… guys are rough," the leader of the Warriors said, still panting while pointing at the orb. "We've got to destroy that thing. It's the source of them. Can we do it?"

Everybody started to cast spells on the orb. Even with everyone's combined power, nothing happened except they saw a nice colorful light-show.

"It's no use," Dani said, "our spells are too weak."

"I recognized that with the lowlifes down there," Salosti said pointing at his remaining scars. "Seems that we can't stop the birth of Kuoles just yet."

"Guess we need more practice."

Salosti turned to face the whole army. Despite the failure to destroy the portal he felt victorious. Overall the first operation of the Last Warriors had been a success. His comrades had suffered a few wounds, but nothing serious. He felt proud.

"Now we have two new members, but Akii, where's your army?"

"They're somewhere else; that was only one portal, and there's dozens of them. We got separated as we were captured."

"Well anyhow, let's go to face Vatarki; I think we're ready with this group," Salosti said.

"Let's go!"

They headed to the town and left the peaceful forest.

Soon, Salosti's army was back in the abandoned school.

"Here we are, Eric! The mission's accomplished, good job!"

Salosti, or anybody else, didn't see Eric anywhere in the school. They called for him and searched everywhere. Salosti found a letter that was addressed to him from Eric.

For Salosti

When you read this I may already be dead.

Yes, I left the building right after you left,

and headed for the Vatarki's castle.

I don't want to be treated like a baby

just because of my age.

This is the deal:

If I come back alive and have beaten

Vatarki, you'll make me your leader;

And if I die you can blame yourself.

Salosti saw Dani walking by him and he concealed the letter in his pocket as quickly as he could. For some reason, he didn't want to tell the others about it.

"Salosti, we couldn't find him; he must've left the building," Dani said.

Salosti only put down his head and whispered silently.

"Yeah, he's gone… I think that we just need to… keep on going."

Dani was puzzled and Salosti ordered everybody to start practicing their fighting skills and magic. The time for their first real battle was almost upon them.

End of Chapter III: Salvation

Chapter IV: Vatarki the First

Salosti's army practiced their skills for two days. They didn't leave the school at any time. Dani shared all the knowledge he had gotten from his parents and teacher in Falgomduza. Each and every one of the Last Warriors getting better, and Salosti noticed the improving. Every night the army made a fire with a spell cast on some wooden desks and other junk found in school to stay warm. They slept in tents that had come along with the camping-set that Dani had bought earlier. Overall their health was well managed, even in such conditions.

Akii still kept on treating King Henrie as if he was still a royal, but the King himself just ignored the care of his former guard. Henrie had always been a beloved king who had ruled Dalik Islands wisely, but ever since he was dethroned he had started considering himself equal with everyone else.

Salosti's perspective about Dani had changed: the Falgomduzian boy was a very nice person, and an invaluable source of knowledge and security. Ferry and David were silent and obeyed every time. They were manly and serious, faithfully respecting every order of their leader. Akii was as nice as always and Henrie was sentimental and not-so-dignified for a king. Actually, Salosti was pretty much pleased with his army, except for Lumi.

Lumi wasn't as cantankerous anymore, but his contemptuous attitude remained. Salosti didn't like Lumi, since the boy was almost perfect opposite to calm Akii. Lumi seemed to like to expiate his earlier fight with Salosti. However, there was no sincerity in his voice or actions. It was more like making a diplomatic relationship for him to get what he wanted.

One night when Salosti was once again fantasying about the day he'd complete his quest and return home, Lumi came to sit by him and started to talk.

"Hi, remember the argument that we had back then in the Underworld? Wow, that was some fight! And I'm… um…" Lumi cleared his throat.

Salosti was anticipating the word "sorry" but was disappointed when he heard Lumi say: "I'm surprised about how strong you're. I mean, no-one else has ever beaten me."

Lumi looked at the floor and played with his hands nervously. Salosti wished that he'd just go away, but he didn't. It was bothersome and awkward, especially with the subject.

"Why are Liisa and Kaste in the army? They are just girls. What can they do?"

"Liisa heard her Order, like you," Salosti replied calmly. It was true; the night before that Liisa had revealed that she had heard her Order during her time in Child Center, and that it was to seek him.

"But the blondie didn't," Lumi continued, about Kaste, "We can kick her out; I mean, there's no use for an extra girl in here, you know? She's just in the way!"

Salosti started to get annoyed, but the tone of his voice didn't change.

"She's Liisa's best friend. She wouldn't approve of her leaving. Besides, there's nowhere for people like us to go. If we're found wandering on the streets we'll just get captured."

Lumi changed the subject.

"Hey, remember that Eric-kid who disappeared. I could tell he was a coward from the start. He probably chickened and ran away to his mother," Lumi laughed. Salosti laughed along reluctantly at the stupid joke. He thought that it was best to be "friends" with Lumi even if he had to do it unwillingly, if he wanted to avoid any troubles.

"Well, good night, pal" Lumi said and walked away. Salosti was relieved to get to resume his alone-time, and got lost in his thoughts again.

Salosti woke up early in the morning. He had seen a horrible nightmare, in which Kuole armies attacked Dalik Islands and got rid of everything and everyone in their way. The capital of the kingdom had already been invaded and the people gotten captured, but it was difficult to tell what had happened to the rest of the kingdom.

Our hero thought that the dream had been an omen, so he decided to not waste any more time at the school. He awakened everybody and started to talk.

"Today we're finally ready to start our second mission: defeating Vatarki. Is everybody ready?"

"I'm tired," Hajosiko said yawning. Salosti ignored him.

"Good! Let's go!"

As usual, Ferry and David were the first ones ready with their armors put on and swords checked. Salosti was a little angry to the rest of the group.

"Come on! You've got to take this seriously, like these two guys. This isn't supposed to be a summer camp!"

Salosti walked by the King of Dalik Islands.

"Sir, are you sure you want to come?"

"Or course! I wanna kick the butts of those fake-kings that shamelessly try to replace us rightful rulers."

Salosti laughed. He hadn't known how fun his majesty was naturally. He walked back to Ferry and David. From Liisa, Kaste and Dani he had heard that Ferry and David had been very strong and helpful during the Operation: Salvation, taking care of most of the enemies in the Underworld. That was why the leader of the Warriors had decided something.

"You guys, I've been thinking a little. When we rescue Akii's army and they join forces with us we can't march in single group anymore or we'll be too noticeable for Kuoles and Raiwox. So I'll split the entire army into three groups; one for each of us."

"Are you serious?" David asked, "You don't even know us that well."

"Why not? You're not the most trustworthy, because I don't know you, but at least you two are the most proper men in the whole army so far. Besides, you two are the oldest-ones if Henrie doesn't count. So, what do you say?"

"It's a deal!" Ferry said.

Salosti ordered his army to head for the castle.

Soon The Last Warriors reached the hill on which the enormous castle stood. Salosti was very nervous and he tried to remember the skills that he had practiced during the two days at abandoned school. "Dodge, slash, cast a spell, guard, help others..."

Everybody else seemed very confident. They withdrew their weapons and were prepared for a demanding fight. Salosti drew out his sword hesitantly: "Let's go," he said with brave voice even though he was afraid and shaking. Vatarki, the tyrant of Unhorimes, was an infamous and merciless man according to mouth word, and nearly everyone who knew him feared him.

Salosti cast a fire-spell on the door. It burned down and they rushed in. There were Tax Ghosts inside. Salosti suspected that they brought the collected taxes to Vatarki; otherwise they shouldn't be inside.

The army avoided the guard-Kuoles and soon found the throne room. There was a glass dome in the middle of the red carpet that led to the golden throne, which was empty. Dani walked by the dome and saw something that was like very fine silvery sand.

"I knew it! He found the crystal dust that gave him special powers," he exclaimed. All the others walked by the dome as well.

"It's so beautiful!" Liisa said.

"But dangerous," Kaste added.

"Let's take it, so he can't use it for anything cruel anymore," Salosti said and tried to lift the dome off.

"FIRE!" someone yelled from the entrance of throne room. Red flames surrounded Salosti's body and he cried out shocked. Hajosiko reacted with a water-spell that he cast on Salosti and extinguished the flames. The army turned around and saw a long-haired bearded man laughing like a maniac. The man looked at Dani and spoke.

"Well, well, if it isn't my younger brother… Dani, was it?"

Dani was mad. For the second time he was facing his brother.

"I thought you had learned after I defeated you back then. Don't even dare to come home after I beat you! You aren't a part of our family anymore!"

"Well, did I come back after I stole Crystals of Falgomduza? NO! So, why would I come back this time?"

Dani didn't answer. He only glared at his brother.

Salosti showed everybody a sign to attack and get the crystal dust. Everybody went in different directions. Salosti dashed to get the dust, Dani went to fight his brother and the rest didn't know what to do.

Salosti cast a thunder-spell on the dome, causing it to shatter. He collected the dust on a leather pouch, and turned around to see what was happening. Just then Vatarki stretched his arm three meters long and punched Salosti in the face. The hero fell backwards and Vatarki took the dust from him and put it in a jar that he made out of nothingness.

The leader of the Warriors saw his whole army fighting against the tyrant, whose arms were made of steel. Vatarki swung his stretchable hands so that Salosti's allies flew against the walls. Salosti tried hopelessly to stop the tyrant king who cast spells like a maniac, but he had forgotten all that he had trained about. He slashed Vatarki with his sword and did some random combos of attacks. He didn't remember any good spells and each time he missed, whether a spell or an attack, Vatarki hit back hard.

Salosti found himself on the floor and he cursed that he had rushed so much. Hajosiko healed him with a cure-spell. He got himself up, raised his head, and saw Dani still fighting Vatarki. The evil brother charged an attack on Dani who blocked it, and counter-attacked. For a moment Vatarki lost his balance; Dani took the chance and cast a wind-spell. Vatarki fell on the floor roughly so that the floor tiles broke. He lost the jar in which the crystal dust was.

Salosti saw the jar flying through the air with great speed. It was about three meters from him. He dove through the air and caught the jar just before it hit the floor. He landed roughly, but was happy that he had saved the jar.

Dani walked by the wounded and powerless Vatarki victoriously.

"Now get out of here," he said, "and never try to conquer anything again, because if you do, I'll always be there to stop you."

Vatarki got on his feet and ran away. His steps echoed in the spacious throne room that was half-broken after the fight. For a moment the throne room was all silent. Then someone said:

"We did it!"

Everybody started to cheer and hug each other, even the normally serious pair of Ferry and David. Salosti was confused; he felt bad that he hadn't really done anything. He only scratched his head and didn't feel the shared happiness like all the others.

"Good job, Salosti!" Dani said smiling and patted his back.

"But I didn't do anything," Salosti said. Then he felt the jar in his pocket and he drew it out.

"Then what's that?" Hajosiko broke in, "Nice save, buddy!"

Salosti started to feel better. Dani took the jar from him.

"I guess the dust is indestructible. We better keep it with us rather than throwing it away. But we won't use it for our own advantage."

Salosti turned to face the entire army: everybody was more or less wounded in battle, but everybody seemed to be okay.

"Come on! Let's celebrate!"

Everybody walked back to the abandoned school and had a party that lasted whole night long.

Vatarki was walking the quiet streets dejected. He had been defeated twice now by a person younger than him. He knew that no matter where he was, his brother would find him and stop his plans. He passed the abandoned school and heard laughing and cheering. He cursed, kicked an empty tin can, and walked away.

End of Chapter IV: Vatarki the First

Chapter V: Top of the World

Salosti woke up late next morning. It was afternoon already. He then remembered the party and sweet victory that they had won yesterday with his men and women. He was happy about his army and even Lumi couldn't spoil this good feeling. He felt that together The Last Warriors could accomplish anything, and get past anything that got on their way.

That day Salosti's army left Unhorimes. Hajosiko was their navigator, for he was the only-one who had a compass and could read a map. The army headed for the capital of Snow Isles, Snow Town.

"The next tyrant-king should be there," Hajosiko said, his eyes fixed on the map, "Only a hundred kilometers to South. Plus we need to cross an ocean, and climb over a mountain and do a few other easy tasks."

The whole army sighed in unison. Then suddenly some Kuoles appeared.

"Well, looks like we're not going to get bored on our travel," Salosti smiled and withdrew his sword.

While Salosti and others were traveling towards Snow Town, we'll see what's going on in another planet, World of Portals.

In WOP, as was the shortened name of the planet, a young man, Tainelm Lehti, lived a boring and hackneyed life of daily and repetitive routines. He lived in the first floor of WOP, the planet of seven completely different floors. Each floor of WOP contained a different world. The people of WOP thought that their world was the whole universe, and that there were no other places anywhere. The only way to get into another floor in WOP was to go through the pipe-elevator that led into the upper floor. The only 'but' was that the pipe-elevator went only upwards, meaning that there was no return to one's home if they decided to go up. That was the reason why most people stayed home; they could never come back if they left, and who knew what horrors could be up there.

One day, Tainelm, an innate adventurer, decided to leave his happy home village. His parents protested.

"You fool! You'll never return. And what if there's nothing up there? What if it only leads you to a worse world?"

Tainelm didn't listen. He had made up his mind to discover the secrets of the world and bring an end to his boring life. From that day on his life would be filled with excitement.

Every villager came to watch when he stepped into the pile-elevator. Even the Mayor of first floor himself came to wish him good journey. Tainelm said his farewells and was gone, like all the others in WOP first floor history that had had the courage to get to the upper floors, and never returned.

Tainelm found himself in the second floor. It was a modern city. It was unlike anything the young man had ever even imagined. He was amazed about the technology and how things worked by pressing a single button. The floating automobiles, all complex electronic devices, and futuristic scenery made him feel dizzy as the first floor had been a small village, close to the nature.

He walked in the city trying to make sense of everything. He was so lost in his thoughts that he accidentally crashed into a girl.

"Oops, pardon me!" Tainelm said and helped the girl up. "Can I ask thy name, young lady?"

The girl giggled: "Why do you speak that way? That's ludicrous!"

Tainelm was mortified.

"From where I am coming from, everybody speaks the way I do."

The girl got excited. "You're from the first floor?"

Tainelm nodded proudly.

"Oh yeah, my name is Wuol. And you?"

Tainelm looked around still amazed about his surrounding new world.

"Tainelm's my name. May I ask, what're all these flying objects? What kind of material do you use to build those amazing machines that obey your orders?"

Wuol explained quickly the basics of the second floor's technology. Apparently a mined element called COF had been found to be charged with energy, and the people of the second floor regulated and distributed that energy to different machines from factories that yielded its power and directed it. Tainelm was puzzled. It all sounded so fantastical to him.

A tall man, dressed in a tux and wearing a top hat, walked by Tainelm and Wuol. He greeted Wuol politely, implying he was an intimate acquaintance. The girl introduced the two men to each other.

"Valo, this is Tainelm; he's from first floor. Tainelm, meet my friend Valo."

Valo shook hands with Tainelm. The latter had never shaken hands before and was confused about the gesture. In his world people greeted each other by having the person of less status kneeling before the other, who would then choose whether or accept them as their new friend. Besides technological differences, the customs of this place seemed to greatly differ from Tainelm's home world.

Valo spoke: "So, Wuol, are you gonna do it today?"

"Well, maybe I will. I'm not sure, but if Tainelm comes along, I would be encouraged," she said, and turned to Tainelm to explain:

"My husband, Wanhaz, a scientist, once went on a journey to see what's on the top of World of Portals. He swore to go all the way to the seventh floor. I thought he was crazy, but now I understand how much I care for him, and I'm going to go to the seventh floor as well. Will you come along with me? You've already gone through the pipe-elevator once, and I'm a little scared to go alone."

Tainelm didn't hesitate; he wanted to see more of the incredible world he had been granted with. He was indeed a man driven by curiosity.

"I am going to go with you till we reach the seventh floor. I want to see the top of the world."

"I'm coming too," Valo said confidently, encouraged by the traveler's determined words..

"All right, let's go already! I can't wait!"

The three excited young adults walked to the pipe-elevator that was in the center of the city. Unlike in the small hometown of Tainelm, the modern city's people did not seem to make such a big deal about someone exiting the place. Perhaps it was more common there. The elevator went upwards with a great speed. Wuol instinctively grabbed Valo's hand to feel more secure. Soon the three reached the third floor.

Tainelm, Valo and Wuol came out at the new world.

"We should check each floor, for Wanhaz could have regretted his trip and stopped halfway through," Valo suggested. It sounded possible, but the friends all also wanted to explore the seven different worlds, so the plan was approved.

The third floor was a green place. There were no people there to be seen. Tainelm felt comfortable in this floor, unlike Valo and Wuol, who had not been accustomed to the lack of buildings, people and machines.

"Why's the sky so darn blue?"

"Why is here so much green?"

"Where're all the people and buildings?"

"What's that transparent quick liquid?"

Now it was Tainelm's turn to explain the way of living in a place that *he* was familiar with. He talked about Mother Nature like she had raised him and taught all of the knowledge like to a disciple. And now that disciple of the green landscape talked vehemently about how strong and fragile, how inconspicuous and essential the environment was.

Wuol was shocked about the explanation.

"So, our floor used to be like this, but we destroyed all the nature with the poisonous steam from the engines of our machines? And we used up so many of the natural resources that it broke the balance of the natural cycle and resulted in the demise of many rare species?"

Tainelm nodded. The girl seemed to be a quick learner. Valo looked around disgusted.

"I still like our floor the better the way it is now."

The three went to the pile-elevator and left the floor of unscathed nature behind.

The fourth floor was an icy place. There was white as far as the eye could see, and the blizzard blew mercilessly. The few locals were Eskimos, living in igloos, who said that most of their neighbors had left the floor in hopes of finding a better home, but some had decided to stay because it was their home. Wuol could somewhat understand how they felt, but Tainelm thought they were just stubborn and naive.

 Nobody of the travelers particularly liked the cold and empty place where all one could hear was the merciless blow of the wind, and there seemed to be nobody. Furthermore, none of them was dressed properly for such a freezing weather, so they left the floor before any of them would catch a cold.

The fifth floor was a city, not as modern as the second floor, but not as green as the third floor. It was a place not too unfamiliar to Tainelm, Valo or Wuol as it combined what had already been seen, and thus was an ideal resting place. The trio was getting tired.

"How about we get a room from an inn, or something?" Valo suggested. Tainelm and Wuol agreed. It had been an exhausting day, and they still had a long way to go.

They found an inn called "Rane's". It was a pretty shaggy place, but the friends had to live with it. Tainelm was the only one who could not sleep. It wasn't because of the bad mattress or the copious rats, but because he was looking forward for the next day. He felt so happy he had found fellow travelers. Making it to the seventh floor would have been much more demanding alone.

In the morning the three adventurers left the fifth floor and went on till they reached the sixth floor.

Tainelm, Wuol and Valo were on the sixth floor. There were many people and the life there seemed to be happy. The place was modern, but in different way than the second floor. This-one seemed even more futuristic and imaginational: The whole world was full of moving and stable floating, transparent panels. Tainelm felt dizzy anytime he looked down through the panel he was standing on and seeing how high above the lower panels he was. The world felt crazy, but the trio enjoyed being there.

Finally after staying in that place for two fun-filled days Tainelm asked when they would go to the final floor, and was shocked to hear that Wuol and Valo had changed their minds.

"No, Tainelm, it's too risky. I've been thinking a little: this sixth floor is still okay, right? But what if the seventh floor is a hell? And you won't ever come back!"

Tainelm felt sad that his friends let him down. He had been thinking the same, but would not let it bother him.

"But, friends of mine, it's not just about reaching the top of the world; it's about the undiscovered secrets and mysteries. If I don't get to know what it is so great or so bad up there I won't get my good-night-sleep ever again. I must discover the unknown. I must know what the prize is for me for working so hard, getting through all the challenges and even abandoning my family to get on this journey. I must know was all this worth doing it."

"Sorry, Tainelm, but I can't risk my life, even if my husband is up there. It probably isn't even worth it."

Tainelm looked down sadly.

"In that case, my friends, I think this be our farewell, for I cannot let friendship be on the way of making my dreams come true."

Tainelm headed for the pipe-elevator and heard both Wuol and Valo yell: "We'll not forget you!" The sole man didn't turn, but kept on going and raised his hand to wave goodbye.

Soon, Tainelm was in the elevator. He had traveled for weeks with his two friends from the second floor, but the time seemed to have gone by so quickly. The final elevator ride went through a pipe that was transparent and Tainelm could see the space, infinite star-ocean. The elevator went on quickly, but to the traveler, the time it took seemed endless; he had seen six unbelievable worlds. They had gotten better and better every time. What would the very last-one be like?

"It must be something that really pops my eyes out", Tainelm thought. He had learned to speak the so-called "normal language" that Wuol and Valo spoke, while hanging around with them. He was very excited to see the seventh floor, but he felt sad that he couldn't share his discovery with anybody else.

Finally, the elevator stopped and Tainelm stepped out. He looked up and saw that the pipe, in which the elevator went, didn't continue any higher. This really was the end of the line, the seventh floor. Tainelm was on The Top of the World.

He observed his surroundings. There was absolutely nobody anywhere. The floor wasn't surrounded by a blue dome like all the other-ones. The entire floor was just an empty panel in the middle of nowhere. Tainelm only saw a curtain of black with little, blinking lights scattered on its surface, like holes. Our hero felt even dizzier than in the sixth floor. He was unsatisfied.

"Is this a joke?" he thought. "Is this reward that I deserve after all I've been through? I lost my home, my family, my friends... all for nothing! The seventh floor was supposed to be heaven or hell, but it's just nothingness! My journey wasn't supposed to have this kind of ending! That's just not fair; I came to seek for the answers, but all I get is nothing but a view of blinking objects in the distance!"

Tainelm sat on the edge of the panel and looked at the beautiful view. It was all just so wrong.

The sole young man spent ten hours sitting at the same spot. Over time he started to respect the view and the seventh floor. With hours of pondering he had figured out his reward:

"Those blinking things must be other worlds! There's so much of them; millions, billions! I came to seek for the answers and I received them. How was I so blind? We, the WOPlings think that there are only seven worlds, the floors of WOP, but in reality our world is only a fraction of piece of dust in a million square-miles! I'm the first-one to discover the truth; that there are other worlds out there; that we're not jailed to live in our villages forever. We can go out there and find a new home! We can live happily and freely without worries of tomorrow. We can solve infinite seas of mysteries and seek for the unknown! We can..."

Tainelm was so excited. He wanted to go out there already, and he wanted to tell his ideas to others; if they only could be there. He thought about all the wasted years that WOP people had spent in their old, boring homes without even knowing that there was a chance to do something new.

Suddenly Tainelm heard voices from the elevator. He saw some strangers that had just come from lower floors. His prayers had been answered!

"What... who... why...?" Tainelm couldn't express his words. There came more and more people from the elevator; dozens of people. Everyone had some packages with them like they were moving. Tainelm recognized some people from the crowds. His parents, Valo and Wuol, and the Mayor of first floor himself had come.

Our hero rushed to his parents.

"What do these people think they're doing? What's going on?"

Tainelm's father spoke.

"Mayor thought that WOP people have been cowards for too long, and encouraged people of each floor to face the truth of seventh floor (most, like us, did), and here we are."

The young man was confused. For decades, or even centuries traveling to the upper floors had been almost a taboo; something that only foolhardy adventurers dared to try. How had the Mayor convinced so many people that it was okay? And why had he had such a sudden revelation of leaving the first floor?

The Mayor seemed as unsatisfied to the seventh floor as Tainelm himself had been at first. So the boy rushed to the Mayor to tell him what the reward of seventh floor really was.

The Mayor became more pleased with the explanation.

"Thank you, son. So, there are other worlds out there, eh? Luckily we packed up everything we had. We should be able to build a ship that can take us somewhere else," he said and turned to face the crowd. He had become the entire planet's leader apparently, as if he was possessing the minds of the other WOPlings. With a loud voice he gave an encouraging speech.

"We didn't know that there were other worlds out there. All the time we've just been stuck in our rotten jail. But now, it's time to make a change! We'll discover the unknown and find a new home!"

The crowd cheered, but then someone asked:

"What if the place we find is inhabited?"

The Mayor thought for a moment. Then he said confidently:

"In that case, we get rid of the inhabitants. We, from whom the truth has been hidden for so long, deserve a new landscape."

The crowd cheered again and people started to gather equipment to build weapons and a space ship that could carry all of them. The best scientists from each floor were directing the process.

Tainelm was happy: he had learned the truth, he'd gotten back his friends and parents, and was about to make his dreams, about revealing the truth about all the other mysteries, come true.

End of Chapter V: Top of the World

Chapter VI: The King of Snow Town

Salosti was in his tent, sleeping during a cold winter night. He had caught a cold and he sneezed frequently. He liked the Snow Isles except it was freezing cold; the temperature was -21 Celsius degrees all day long. The army's travel had been rough: battles against Kuoles were getting even more common, food was running out, and the camping-set was getting ragged with the weather conditions.

The leader of the Warriors had received a magical letter from both David and Ferry. They had left the army a couple days ago to lead two other armies with Akii's men, whom the Last Warriors had rescued on their way to Snow Isles. It had been fairly easy to rescue the Royal Army from the Underworld, and since Salosti was a man of his word, he had split Akii's army into two groups, and gave authority of each to David and Ferry.

Both letters were about how happy the two fellow leaders were to get to lead their own armies. Salosti had sent Ferry's army to Hallow Isles and David's army to Light Isles. Their jobs were to fight against Kuole armies, destroy portals, and set the two other original kings free from the underworld. Meanwhile Salosti's army would fight against the two remaining tyrant-kings.

The travel from Unhorimes to Snow Isles had made The Warriors much stronger, but also each and everyone extremely tired.

Salosti came out of his tent and looked around the camp. Hajosiko, Kaste and Akii were sitting around the fire to stay warm, Dani was sharpening his sword, King Henrie was slumbering in a sleeping bag, snoring loudly, Liisa was weaving something out of wool, and Lumi leaned against a tree and let the snow-flakes fall into his mouth.

It was snowing and it was so cold that the breath turned into steam. Dani got an idea of that, picked a stick and put it in front of his mouth. Then he blew out some steam, imitating a smoking person. Everybody laughed; even Salosti. He was still a little jealous of Dani who made everybody feel so comfortable and safe.

Salosti walked by Akii and sat beside him.

"I think that we need something to help us travel faster and easier in this place," Salosti said.

"Agreed," Akii replied. "The blizzard is pretty hard."

"Skis would be great," Hajosiko broke in. "Or snow shoes."

"If there only was a shop where we could buy ones," Kaste said. There were not many buildings in Snow Isles, much less shops. The whole island was merely a white, snowy mountain with huge spruces everywhere.

Hajosiko read his map thoughtfully.

"The whole Snow Town seems to be inside the king's castle," he said puzzled and turned the map upside-down, "I've heard that Snow Town's full of nice people; maybe we can find some to our army."

None of the warriors had ever visited the Snow Town, so they were excited to get to see it imminently. Another rumor besides the one about people being nice there was that the town had amazing food.

Liisa walked by the fire holding wooly clothes that she had made by hand.

"Here! These should keep you guys warm," she said and gave a pair of soft and warm gloves for everyone. They thanked her, all except for Lumi.

Dani finished polishing his sword and came to sit by the fire next to Liisa.

"Maybe we can build our own skis," he suggested. "Like this," he said and picked up a piece of wood and started carving it with a pocketknife. All the others started to do the same, and all the skis were ready in the morning. Although they were far from perfect, and Lumi and Hajosiko had cut their fingers, the skis were good enough to make the traveling easier.

The army packed up the camping-set, set out the fire and headed for the bright Snow Town that was still eleven kilometers away. Everybody put on their new handmade skis. Dani, Salosti and Akii were the only ones that were good skiers. They acted as leaders of the group, and guided the others who were less skilled. The warriors were on top of a mountain, in the height of five kilometers from the ground. They started to go downhill skiing down the snowy mountain; it didn't go very well.

Liisa crashed on a tree. Salosti helped her out and she was very embarrassed.

"I'm sorry for the inconvenience," she said when the leader of the warriors was pulling her up. "I must really be slowing you guys down."

"It's okay," Salosti said with a smile, and brushed some snow off from the top of Liisa's head. For some reason the gesture made her blush. "The others aren't doing much better."

Lumi couldn't control where he was going and he went the wrong way, tripped and his skis flew away. Akii went to get him back. Hajosiko couldn't even stand on the skis; Dani went to guide him.

Finally everybody was going down the snowy mountain somehow. Salosti, who hadn't gone in such a speed for quite a while felt his adrenaline rush and went to ski next to Akii.

"Hey, I'll race you!" He yelled over the other voices with a self-confident grin.

"You're on!" Akii yelled back and boosted himself to a high speed with his ski sticks.

"Hey, you cheated… ah, whatever," Salosti muttered to himself and raised his speed as well. He felt the speed and blizzard lambasting his face. He went faster and faster until he reached a bare part of the mountain that didn't have snow on it, but only black ice. It came as a complete surprise to him. Just seconds ago he had been on a thick layer of snow.

Salosti had lost Akii from his sight and he was shocked. He tried to brake, but he was going too fast and had already reached the black ice, and was about to slip.

"If I fall on my head now, I'll die," Salosti thought and tried to keep his balance. "I cannot let it end this way. They all trust me. This is no honorable way for the leader of the warriors to die, especially since the quest isn't even nearly completed." The bald part ended and Salosti was relieved that he was back on nice, soft, and safe snow layer. He had just been in a mortal danger.

Now Salosti was able to stop, and he did. He looked around and searched for his army. He saw then Akii coming down from another direction and stopping beside him.

"How the heck did you get here before me?" Akii asked amazed.

"I hope I didn't! I almost died," Salosti replied, still shocked about the situation. He explained the bald part that he had crossed, to Akii.

"Whoa, no more races or any kind of kidding," Akii said seriously, glad that his friend hadn't been hurt.

The two heard voices from somewhere higher. Then they saw their army being chased by Kuoles. These ones were not the common Kuoles that the army faced daily; these ones wore armors and had weapons.

"Ski for your lives," Dani yelled over the thunder. Akii and Salosti turned around and exploded to high speed. The group separated and Salosti found himself alone in the middle of a hill full of trees. He had to slalom them. He heard machine-gun sounds and looked back; some armed enemies were behind him, trying to shoot him.

"How the hell did they get those weapons? That technology was banned decades ago!"

Salosti avoided the gunshots and trees, and skid as fast as he could. Finally, when he reached the end of the mountain, he heard a loud thunder of billowing masses of snow; it was an avalanche!

Trees were buried under the layers of raging snow wave. Salosti was in panic. He made a strong magical shield around himself and prepared to die. The avalanche went over Salosti's magical shield-orb and it was buried. All he could see now was dark.

He waited inside his shield-orb until he heard no more the rumbling of the avalanche. Then he came out and immediately started casting fire-spells. Some of the snow around him melted, but there still was a three meters thick snow-layer on him.

Finally he reached the surface and started to call his friends. He found Akii who had acted the same way as he had. They found the rest of the army surprisingly quickly. Everybody seemed to be okay. Salosti was relieved. He felt like he was to blame for being an inconsiderate and leaving his army.

"I'm sorry," he said, "that was all my fault; I shouldn't have gone by myself like that."

Dani walked by him and gave him a friendly punch on the side.

"That's okay, cheer up! That was actually kinda fun!"

Salosti nodded even though he didn't agree. He didn't like these "that-was-too-close situations". The Warriors continued their travel without skis, as they had been either buried or destroyed. Thanks to the speed they had provided, though, nobody had been harmed by the new kinds of Kuoles. Salosti still wondered why they looked so different than before. When the leader asked aloud Dani said with concern:

"I tried to stop them with a few spells, but they were much stronger than the Kuoles we have encountered so far. Also, their attacks were much harder to block."

"Well, at least we outran them," Hajosiko said optimistically.

Suddenly Liisa stopped on her tracks and hugged Kaste, who was walking next to her.

"I was so worried you might get killed," she said with tears in her eyes, "I was trying not to lose sight of you, but I couldn't control where I was going. I'm sorry…"

"Calm down, Liisa," Kaste said comfortingly, "It's over now. I'm not gonna die that easily and leave you alone."

"Promise?"

"Promise."

Salosti smiled to himself. He saw Lumi rolling his eyes, but did not care. He was happy that most of his comrades cared for each other. Without such bonds the teamwork would not function as well as it did. Fights had been won against Kuoles with the power of friendship, and so would the quest continue.

Finally the army reached Snow Town. It was inside the king's castle like Hajosiko had told earlier. The castle was huge; much bigger than the one that was in Unhorimes (obviously, since it was supposed to fit a whole town in it). The castle was made of ice, or at least looked like it. Hajosiko told the others that it moved around every now and then to a different spot on the Snow Isles, because it was sort of like an artificial animal that moved to colder places when it got too warm in its current location.

The group was having a trouble figuring out how to get in. They had found the entrance, but the door was locked and seemed to be immune to all kinds of magic. The army had already given up trying to get in when Akii came up with an idea.

"Why don't we just wait here outside till somebody comes out of the door? Then we can quickly get in before the door gets closed again."

The plan sounded like it would work and nobody else had any bright ideas, so the army decided to go with it. They started waiting.

Finally someone came outside using the door. Salosti's army was prepared and stopped the door from closing. Then they all got inside. There wasn't any snow in there, so Salosti wondered why the town was named Snow Town. But it was surrounded by snow of course, he reminded himself.

Salosti wondered where the king might be. The people of Snow Town were salesmen in markets and bazaars. Everybody seemed unhappy, probably because of the cruel rules of the tyrant.

"So, where do you guys suppose the tyrant-king of this town is hiding?" Salosti asked.

"Maybe we can ask the citizens," Hajosiko suggested and walked by a random person who was running a shop.

"Excuse me sir, but do you happen to know where the King of Snow Town is?" Hajosiko asked politely. The person was startled, either because of the question or because he recognized the asker's face and companions. At any rate, he raised his arm that was made of steel and pressed a button on it.

Suddenly there came a loud beeping noise everywhere and an announcement: "Warning: invaders at the South-gate!" that repeated itself many times.

Salosti and the others withdrew their weapons. Some guard-looking Kuoles appeared.

"Let's separate!" Dani yelled and everybody ran off to different directions.

Some of the citizens panicked, some started chasing Salosti's friends, trying to stop them. The whole Snow Town was in chaos and the voices echoed in the castle.

Salosti was running in a bazaar. Some armed citizens tried to shoot him, but he shielded himself, so that the gunshots reflected back to them. The brave warrior set the whole bazaar on fire with a powerful fire-spell, turned his shield-orb into a water-orb, and continued running. His trick made him get rid of all his chasers.

He was still worrying about the rest of his army as he stopped to catch his breath.

Suddenly, all the voices in Snow Town were gone. A screen in the castle's ceiling appeared, a maniac-looking man with a crown in it. His voice came from all the loudspeakers, echoing in the castle.

"Intruders, whoever you are, if you don't come into my throne room unarmed, holding a white flag, you'll pay with the lives of the innocent people in this town. I'll give you ten, I repeat, ten minutes to come here. And don't even think to try anything stupid; all four gates are blocked!"

The screen disappeared and the worried voices came back to the castle. Salosti found himself in somebody's store that was now ruined. He came out and started to search for his army, wishing that they were all right. Now he understood why the citizens had attacked them. Their king wasn't afraid of sacrificing innocents if someone antagonized him. They were forced to pick a side, although either way they were doing something evil to someone else. The second tyrant was obviously even crueler than Vatarki had been.

Salosti finally found Dani. The other boy wasn't alone; he was hugging Liisa and seemingly enjoyed himself. Perplexed and angry, Salosti tore the two apart and started yelling at Dani out of jealousy.

"What do you think you're doing? This isn't the time or place for romance; we're in the middle of an emergency situation. Didn't you hear what that lunatic just announced?"

Dani seemed embarrassed and confused, but yelled back angrily.

"Be quiet, comrade!" he came close to Salosti and whispered to his ear "She just lost her best friend."

"Kaste?" Salosti whispered shocked. Dani nodded. Salosti now looked at Liisa and saw that she was crying.

"Where's she?" our hero asked quietly from Dani.

The Falgomduzian pointed at a window of a shop. Salosti saw Kaste's dead body behind the broken window. The girl's left arm was gone and her stomach was full of bloody holes; she had been killed by one of her chasers who had shot her.

"This is horrible! What are we gonna do now?" Salosti asked from Dani.

"I was about to ask you the same," Dani replied "I think that we should do as the tyrant wants. We can't let the innocent people die."

"Okay, but are we going to find the others first so we can all go together?"

"No, it takes too long and we don't have much time. We better go now, just the two of us," Dani said and took a piece of white fabric and tied it on a stick to represent the white flag. "We have the advantage that he doesn't know how many of us are here. When we two go in, he won't hurt anyone, and if he tries to do something with us, we'll at least have the rest of the army safe."

"Is Liisa coming with us?" Salosti asked.

"I think that it's better if she stays," Dani answered. The other boy nodded compassionately.

Salosti and Dani headed for the castle. The map to reach it was in the screen hanging on the ceiling. The throne room was in a tower that was in the center of Snow Town.

"How are we gonna return the original king of Snow Town to his throne if we give up on this guy?" Salosti wondered. "All the tyrants must be slain or at least overthrown."

Dani had thought the same already.

"We'll think about that later. The lives of the citizens are our first priority now."

The two warriors reached the throne room- tower. They marched in, keeping their hands in the air. The man with a mad glare, the tyrant of Snow Town, was sitting on the throne. He laughed at the two. Both were angry and felt awkward and naked. The door behind them closed on its own.

"Mwahahahaa!" the maniac laughed. "Did you think that I would spare your lives even if you gave up? Wrong! I will kill you anyway! No one who threatens my power like you shall stay alive in this world!"

The tyrant drew out a rifle.

"Can't any of you bums use magic in here?" Dani questioned the tyrant. He was starting to miss the unarmed Kuoles.

"Bah! Who needs magic, when you can make things destroyed faster and easier?" the tyrant replied. He obviously had never learned magic. "Okay, no more talking! Under the orders of Raiwox, I will annihilate The Last Warriors of Light here and now!"

The tyrant started shooting. Salosti and Dani leaped out of the way just in time. Both withdrew their weapons out of the thin air. The tyrant was amazed.

"WHAT! You weren't supposed to have any weapons, you cheaters! You're using magic; that's not fair!"

Dani and Salosti smiled at each other and started fighting the maniac.

Suddenly Salosti's army rushed into the throne room with some rebellious citizens who seemed to be allying them. Salosti was happy to see his friends okay, but he was also worried that the cruel tyrant would hurt them.

"Watch out; he's armed!"

When Hajosiko made a strong spell on the tyrant, he lost his rifle.

The maniac went completely insane; he drew out two laser guns from his pockets and started shooting randomly everywhere while laughing self-confidently. The people shielded themselves, but one of the shots hit Hajosiko's shoulder.

Salosti saw frightened from the side how the maniac shot two innocent citizens to their deaths. Rage awakened within him. He sneaked behind the maniac when he was focusing on other warriors, and jumped in his back. He tried to reach for the guns in the maniac's hands. He caught one and hit the tyrant's face with it several times. The cruel king cried out of pain and shot many times in random directions with his remaining gun. Salosti finally caught the other gun and threw it away. The maniac was squirming on the ground, bleeding.

Salosti turned around to yell at his army.

"Help me get him while we can!"

The others surrounded the tyrant that didn't move anymore. Salosti got up on his feet, shaking, sweating and panting. He joined the circle around the tyrant.

Hajosiko spoke like a police officer.

"Get on your feet and put your hands up! Don't make any sudden moves; you're surrounded."

The man didn't move at all. The army waited for a moment. Lumi broke the silence.

"Salosti, you killed him!" he said more like excited than shocked. Salosti felt sick. He spoke with a shaky voice.

"I… I didn't mean to. I tried to protect..."

Akii walked by him and patted his shoulder, a true friend that he was.

"It's okay. He was only a tyrant, like Raiwox."

Salosti nodded. Suddenly he felt someone hugging him. Salosti looked down and saw that it was Liisa.

"I was worried sick about you," she said and made Salosti forget about everything for a moment.

"Me too," said Hajosiko.

"Me three," said someone else. The whole army admitted that they had been worried about each other.

The shared happiness made Salosti feel like he had a family. As an orphan, the feeling was new to him and he wanted to preserve it. He wanted to share his life with these people forever. They were the best friends he could ask for.

With help of Hajosiko, Salosti made himself talk in the screen for the citizens, his voice coming from the loudspeakers.

"Hello, citizens! The tyrant of this down is dead now. You do not have to bear the unfairness anymore in this town, nor will you live in a constant fear. I will continue my journey for the freedom of good people, so farewell, my friends."

Salosti ended his speech and walked outside with his army. The crowd was cheering and everybody wanted to celebrate. Salosti and the others received a free stay at a five-star hotel. They celebrated whole night long, eating, dancing and doing fun activities. The party at Unhorimes was nothing compared to this-one.

In the morning, Salosti and the others left the Snow Town and changed their course to their next destination.

End of Chapter 6: The King of Snow Town

Chapter VII: The Dead Garden

Finally the first ships of WOP had blasted away to the space. All the people didn't fit in the same ship, so all of them couldn't go at the same time, but the Mayor gave Tainelm the honor to be in the first ship with him, thanks to his intelligent deductions about outside worlds.

The first ship reached the surface of an unknown planet. They were on Earth, the planet their ancestors had left long ago. It was immediately noticed that the planet was inhabited when they saw all the buildings. They saw no people, though. The Mayor said thoughtfully:

"We are going have to get rid of the aliens that inhabit this planet. But we've got to test them before we tell the others to come."

Tainelm felt that something was wrong.

"Aren't we the aliens in this case? And sir, why can't we all just live together?" He asked.

"There's no way that the aliens are gonna let us take over their planet. It's morally right, though, because the truth's been hidden from us for so long. We deserve to get a new home. We've been tricked."

Tainelm still disagreed, but said nothing.

The Mayor gave an order for his underlings to come out of the ship. They came out and Tainelm saw what they wore: armored suits made of some alloy, with rifles and bazookas in their arms. They were going to invade Earth.

Salosti and the others came out of the Snow Town after mourning in Kaste's funeral. They traveled under the aurora and starlight, leaving the coldness of Snow Isles. Hajosiko tried to navigate their way to their next destination; Mas Town, the home of the last tyrant-king. All the kids and King Henrie had heard of Mas Town, which was also known as Crisis Town because of all the criminals that were causing confusion there. Salosti wished that nobody would get killed or even hurt there. Kaste's death had been heartbreaking enough. None of the warriors could probably handle another loss.

The army made a camp in a humid swamp in a rainforest. Lumi whined that his shoes were all wet. Hajosiko had to admit that he wasn't sure where they were. King Henrie had caught a cold and Akii took care of him. Liisa had been silent for a while. Ever since her best friend's death, she had started secluding herself. Hajosiko wasn't with her anymore, like he used to be. Dani was like he always appeared; telling jokes and cheering up others. Salosti started to like him more now that he was used to him.

Salosti lay in his sleeping-bag inside his tent. He was thinking what the third tyrant would be like. The past two had been very rough and had caused serious injuries to his friends. He was happy that Dani and Hajosiko were such good Supporters, healing the wounded Attackers and Defenders.

Suddenly, there came a shriek from outside. Salosti got alarmed and dashed outside, thinking of a Kuole army. He saw only Akii, shaking over Hajosiko, who was lying on the ground in his feet. Everybody else came out of their tents.

"He's dead!" Someone shouted.

Dani walked beside Hajosiko's dead body and examined him.

"He's been killed by a powerful spell or pierced by a sword," he said turning to face the others. Everybody looked at each other.

"Somebody here's a traitor," Salosti said. "Because Kuoles don't assassinate single persons like that. When they attack, they don't care if they are noticed."

The leader was depressed that he had lost another one of his friend so quickly.

Liisa didn't cry, though everybody thought she did as she was drooping her head. She gloomily walked towards Lumi and cast a thunder-spell on him all of a sudden. Lumi flinched and paralyzed. Liisa withdrew her swords, but Akii dashed to hold her back.

"You killed him! You're the traitor; I know it!" She yelled, struggling to get free.

Lumi was still confused.

"No, no… it wasn't me, I swear…" he tried to explain.

Akii loosened his grip of Liisa, who immediately dashed towards Lumi.

"STOP!" Salosti shouted and everybody stopped. "We have no proof that he's the traitor," he continued "I can be the traitor, anyone can be! There's no sense if we blame somebody without a proof…"

Dani interrupted him:

"Well, do you suggest that we just go back to sleep and wait till someone else gets murdered by the traitor? We must find that person now, or we'll all get killed!"

Salosti started to think. He had his guess about the traitor, but decided not to make sudden decisions.

"How about this: two of us will stay awake, on guard by the fire, while the others are sleeping." Others thought that it was fair. "Okay, who volunteers to stay awake with me tonight?" He asked.

King Henrie volunteered even though he was sick. He thought that it would help his cold if he was near the warm fire all night.

So, Salosti and Henrie sat by the fire, and the rest went back to their tents. Henrie started talking.

"How's it going, son? Is everything all right?" He asked kindly.

"Yeah, I think so. Why?"

"Because I'm worried that you work too hard," said the king.

Salosti was confused.

"Since when have you worried about me, sir?"

"I always have. I want you to be as happy as possible."

"Well, thanks, sir, but I don't think I need any kind of help," Salosti said and raised his head to see the starry sky.

The leader soon noticed that he had almost fallen asleep while he was thinking about the last tyrant. He tried to get a hold of himself. He saw that the king opposite to him was sleeping.

"Sir, we're supposed to stay awake," Salosti said shaking Henrie.

King Henrie got on his feet and slapped himself on the cheeks. He took a canteen and poured water all over his clothes. Then he shook himself dry like a dog and said: "Okay, I'm ready."

Salosti and King Henrie sat around the fire for a long time. Both were about to fall asleep all the time. Every time when Salosti noticed that he was leaning against something, he raised his body up and pinched himself. He even scratched himself with his dagger sometimes. The king talked half-asleep.

"Salosti, what would you do to me if I was the traitor? Would you kill me?"

Salosti was puzzled about the sudden, weird question.

"No, I wouldn't, because I'd still have to return you to your throne in order to make it to the Middle Island. If you weren't an original king and you were the traitor, I'd kill you. I won't forgive the one who deprived the lives of two of my friends. But why'd you ask that, sir?"

The king answered Salosti's question indirectly.

"I wouldn't kill you even if you were the traitor. But I can't help... I..." the king didn't finish his sentence. Salosti reached out his head to see his face and saw that he was sleeping. The boy didn't dare to wake him up again, so he had to stay awake the whole night without any company.

Salosti woke up late in the morning. He had fallen asleep. He cursed, but was relieved to see the army on the whole (or what was left of it): Dani, King Henrie, Lumi, and Akii were all okay. Salosti didn't see Liisa anywhere, but was sure that she was still sleeping.

He walked to his tent and saw two magical letters addressed for him. Salosti read the first-one that was from Liisa.

Hey, Salosti

I'm sorry for leaving so soon and without saying goodbye,

but I got a message from home.

It was my mother; she isn't too well. She is suffering a disease,

so I traveled to Unhorimes to see her and my brother.

I really wish I can get back soon!

Liisa

Salosti read Liisa's letter and put it on the side. He grabbed the other letter which was from David and Ferry.

SALOSTI

We're in a trouble; not only armies of Kuoles are rampaging, but now even aliens from outer space (WOP) are invading this planet! The aliens are wearing metallic armors and use guns. Beware; they're even worse than Kuoles. The aliens can fly with their armors among other things that WILL cause problems when fighting them.

So, now Kuoles and aliens are fighting against our small armies. We've heard that next, the aliens are gonna attack Unhorimes. We can't afford to lose that post at this point, because it's like our headquarters.

We hope that your army will get here soon, so now you must delay your mission a little.

Ferry and David

Salosti was shocked after he read the letter:

"Damn! There's gonna be a war at Unhorimes, and Liisa just went there to visit her mom! She's completely unaware and unprepared." Salosti came out of his tent and walked by Dani.

"We've gotta change the course to Unhorimes. There's gonna be a big battle, and Liisa's there with her family."

Salosti let Dani read both letters. The other boy was frightened as well, but not for the same reason.

"You're right, Salosti! If we don't stop the aliens now, they'll definitely send the rest of them here, and outnumber us."

Lumi protested as usually; this time for a good reason.

"This sucks! We traveled all this way towards Mas Town, and just when we're about to reach it, we've got to turn back."

"I kinda agree with Lumi," Dani admitted "There's no sense if we go all the way there; we can't do much in the battle. We've got only-" he counted the people remaining in the army, "five people left; minus the traitor, so it's four! It can't depend on us!"

King Henrie walked by the four, Akii hurrying after him yelling: "Sir, you're still not supposed to get outta your bed."

The king looked around in the camp with a deadpan face.

"It may be true that we haven't got much people," he glared especially at Lumi and Dani. "But my opinion is that I've never had fighters this good even among my Royal Knights!"

Everybody except for Lumi, cheered for the encouragement. Now that Hajosiko was gone, Akii did the navigating for him. The army headed for Unhorimes after burying Hajosiko and celebrating his memory. Salosti swore that he would definitely kill the traitor, whoever it was.

On the way to Unhorimes, the army faced many troubles: the king was still sick and his couches started to sound critical. Kuoles seemed to lurk behind every corner. Raiwox was getting really mad, since two of the tyrants had been defeated, so he increased the taxes and sizes of his armies. Salosti's worst fear was that aliens- their new enemy- would team up with Kuoles. "That's probably what Raiwox will try to do," he thought. "An alliance that would put us Warriors into trouble."

The army figured how desperate it would be if their two enemies would ally together against The Last Warriors of Light. Dani got an idea how they could get a little help: he sent a magical letter to Falgomduza, and asked for help while threatening that if Earth was to be invaded, Falgomduza would be next. The beg for help was not going against his Order; he had not taken anyone with him when leaving his home planet. Nothing stopped him from asking for help from Earth. So, some people from Falgomduza went on a journey around the sun to reach the planet in chaos; Earth. After all, Dani was the one who had saved them once from Vatarki.

Salosti, Akii, King Henrie, Lumi, and Dani had traveled for three days. They were resting in an inn in a dark city that was in Dalik Islands region. Dani was now completely out of money.

"Enjoy your last night under a roof," he said. "Because from now on we must sleep under the stars all the time *without* our camping-set; it's all broken, so you can't sleep in tents anymore."

The atmosphere in the dark room was gloomy. Nobody was excited to sleep in the cold. And from experience everybody knew that the travel to Unhorimes had just begun. Salosti knew that he was near his old home, but somehow he didn't feel like it. Somehow the excitement of returning after victory didn't taste so sweet anymore. Suddenly his army wasn't a family anymore; just bunch of some slayers of dark creatures. The dream of beating Raiwox seemed worthless, and Salosti didn't know what he wanted anymore. He was confused; something was missing. What could it be?

Everybody remained silent. Salosti hoped that Dani would start to tell his jokes, but he didn't. All seemed so dark, so spiritless. Salosti remembered how amazed he had been when he saw magic for the first time. Now he possessed magical skills, but still, they seemed as ordinary as daily talking. Also the blue sky outside seemed to have turned into an everlasting black. The Earth wasn't colorful anymore; no more sunlight, no more aurora, no more starry sky, no more anything. All the magic seemed to be gone.

"We can't go on like this," Salosti said thoughtfully. Everybody turned to face him "We've gotta move faster. From now on we'll run without stopping all day long. So, now I suggest we'll all get some zesty sleep so we'll all be spry tomorrow."

Everybody went to sleep.

The five woke up early next morning and left the inn. They started running. Dani saw a flycycle (flying bicycle that works with steam engine) shop. Everybody wanted to have some vehicles firstly, because their legs were tired, secondly, because it would be faster.

"Let's steal ones!" Lumi said. "We'll use them for good."

Salosti agreed with Lumi for the first time in his life.

"You're right! It's not bad if we commit a minimal crime to save Earth."

Everybody sneaked by the shop and picked one flycycle for each person. King Henrie was excited.

"Boy, I haven't done this since I was a rascal."

The army started traveling with the flycycles. Everyone was able to ride.

"See? I told you it's easier if we don't have girls!" Lumi said to Salosti.

The traveling went much more quickly than it had lasted when they had gone by foot. Soon the army was only few kilometers from Unhorimes.

They saw lights and heard gun sounds. Some buildings were on fire.

"We're late!" Salosti said. "The battle has begun!"

They left their flycycles because the hill that led to the town was too steep to ride down. Everybody withdrew their weapons and prepared for a battle. They separated and started searching for David's and Ferry's armies from the seas of Kuoles and invaders.

Liisa had finished crying. She wiped her tears from her cheeks and went to look for something sharp from her house. She found a knife and she picked it up confidently yet fearfully. "Forgive me, Salosti," she thought.

Suddenly, the door slammed wide open. Liisa couldn't see who was standing at the door in the darkness. It was raining hard outside and a lightning struck. During the flash Liisa saw the round, metal covered person at the door.

"Who's there? Is it you mother?" Liisa asked hopelessly.

She heard the figure laugh like a maniac and saw the crown in its head flash. The person raised a rifle pointing at Liisa.

"Mother! Someone! HELP!" She shrieked and her screams drowned into the thunder crashes. Only the maniacal laughter remained.

Salosti dashed towards an army that was mixture of Kuoles and armored soldiers. He was not sure if they were allies or fighting against each other, but didn't have time to think. He unleashed a whirling slash while turning his sword into fiery lava stick with a fire-spell. The enemies around him disappeared and more appeared to replace them. There didn't seem to be any empty spots on the battlefield.

The aliens were much stronger than the Kuoles, and when they died, they whether exploded in fire and flames or paralyzed and fell to remain on the ground. Salosti couldn't see the faces of the aliens because of the masks they wore. The aliens didn't appear out of nowhere like Kuoles; they were dropping down from the skies with parachutes. Some aliens flew in the air with their jetpacks. Most of them were armed with guns, others had disc saws and flamethrowers equipped with them.

Even though the aliens and Kuoles were outnumbering Salosti's, David's and Ferry's armies, they caught them up. Salosti had to shield himself all the time for gunshots. Unfortunately his magical powers felt weak just that moment. And not only his magic; his whole spirit seemed depressed. Somehow he already knew that the battle was lost.

It was morning, but the sky remained black. Salosti and the Warriors had won the battle. There were only few aliens and Kuoles left. The rest had either died or fled. It was raining silently. Salosti remembered Liisa and decided to go look for her now that the battle was over. He didn't have the least idea where she could live, so he decided to check all the houses.

Unhorimes was full of broken buildings and cars, cheering and fighting people, and grayness. The entire town seemed to have turned to gray. It was like a movie on slow-motion. Salosti kept on looking for Liisa's house.

A weird looking house with a magical garden hit the hero's eye. He decided to check it. The garden was the only place in the entire town that had any colors. It was very colorful, full of beautiful purple plants. However, the garden was half-dead. The dead part was as grey as the town. Salosti walked through the garden and reached a backdoor. He saw a gun on the doormat. He picked it up and put in his pocket just in case; his magic was getting too weak to use for fighting, so he needed something else to protect himself with if someone attacked him. He walked in and saw the house from inside. It was all ruined: the walls were pierced, doors splintered, and some places were on fire. The hero extinguished the flames on his way.

Salosti saw a light in the dark house coming from one of the rooms. He walked inside the room. It was white and he could see a bed surrounded by flowers, Liisa lying on it, her eyes closed. The warrior gasped. He saw a young man beside the bed. That man held a knife in his hand. Salosti's heart started to beat extremely fast; he noticed that Liisa wasn't breathing.

"Liisa, I'm so sorry!" the young man sobbed. Salosti stepped inside the room and took the gun from his pocket.

"Why'd you kill her? Who are you?" Salosti asked quickly and angrily. The man turned around and was shocked.

"Who are you? Get out, this is my house! GET OUT!" He yelled.

Salosti didn't move except he raised his gun callously to point at the man. The man raised his hands up and cried:

"Spare me! This isn't what it looks like, I swear. I'm begging you, don't kill…"

Salosti pulled the trigger: **BOOM!** The man fell on the floor dead. Salosti was shaking and walked by the bed. Liisa still wasn't breathing; she was dead.

The boy felt absolutely hollow. Three of his childhood friends had died, and he felt like he was to blame. He thought that he could have saved them if he had been quick enough.

Salosti saw a letter in Liisa's table. He picked it up and read it:

Jones

You're the only one I got left in our family, dear brother.

Our mother's dead, I don't know about father,

I heard that he escaped.

Please don't die at Battle for Unhorimes.

I'm afraid that I'll have to be alone again.

If you're alive and read this letter, please join

Salosti's army.

He can protect you as he protected me.

If you find him, please tell him that I'll come back

And that my heart will always belong to him.

Liisa

Salosti didn't know what to think. He had just killed Liisa's brother; the only survivor of her family. He squeezed the letter and tore it to dozens of pieces. He took the fatal gun and threw it away. He walked out of the building and promised to obliterate the one responsible for Liisa's death. He heard the people celebrating the victory of Battle for Unhorimes, but he didn't feel like celebrating. Endless tears were falling down his cheeks.

As Salosti walked through the garden again, he noticed that it was now all dead, since Liisa's whole family that had kept its magic up, was gone. Salosti left the dead, gray garden knowing that all the magic from the world was gone as the magic of the garden had died away.

End of Chapter VII: The Dead Garden

Chapter VIII: The Traitor

As Salosti walked through the town, he came up with a horrific idea: he decided to leave his army, his mission, everything that was ordered in the destiny of mankind, written in stars. Suddenly, a big longing for home had stricken the young man. He wanted to go home and forget about his contemptible journey that had lasted for three months. Only three months ago he had been in his sweet home without worries about tomorrow. His homelessness didn't bother him; at least he could forget about the daily worries of army life. He was extremely tired after the battle and the shocking scene at the house of dead garden. And he was sick of seeing his loved ones die one by one.

When Salosti remembered about the horror of the white room, he started shaking again and tried to prevent himself from crying. It was hard, though.

Akii, Dani, Lumi and King Henrie were searching for Salosti. Each of them was in fairly good shape after the Battle. Their teamwork had saved them.

"I'm sorry that I lost you from my sight, sir! I promised to protect you, and I failed! It's my fault," Akii apologized humbly to King Henrie. His master didn't seem mad at all.

"Don't worry! I enjoyed fighting alone. I got a lot done!" King Henrie replied his eyes blinking. Akii did not believe his eyes; was it blinking of madness in his majesty's eyes? Akii suspected that his master had done something unusual.

The group saw a stranger in the distance. She was a young woman who obviously wasn't a local. She seemed to be lost.

"Can we help you, miss?" Akii asked politely. Wuol turned around and came closer to the group.

"Has any of you heard of a person called Wanhaz? He's my husband and I've been hopelessly looking for him for ages... Have you heard of him?"

"Uh, no..." everybody muttered.

"Okay... Thanks anyway..." She said disappointed. Since her fiancé had not been in the seventh floor of WOP, she had hoped to find him in another planet.

Wuol turned around and walked away from the group, probably crying, and left the army to the dark, empty city in an awkward silence.

"Well, that was weird! I wonder what her problem was," Lumi said stupidly, breaking the silence. Dani slapped the top of Lumi's head for all the people in the army.

Salosti walked up a hill on which stood an empty cottage, near to the forest. He decided to rest there and to go home in the morning. He heard somebody running towards him from behind. He withdrew his sword and turned around, preparing to fight. It was only his army.

"Oh, you guys," Salosti said tiredly, turned around, and continued going up the hill. Dani, King Henrie, Akii and Lumi hurried to walk beside him on a line, obediently waiting for his orders.

"So, now it's to the Mas Town, eh, buddy?" Akii said. "But first we gotta celebrate our victory, of course!"

Salosti made himself walk quicker. He didn't want to talk right that moment, because he was afraid that he'd burst into tears in front of his army.

"Come on, Salosti, where are you going?" Dani asked.

"Home" Salosti replied quickly. Dani laughed reluctantly, thinking it was supposed to be a bad joke.

"Haha! Good one!" He said and turned serious again "But seriously, where you going?"

The army got left behind. Everybody sensed that something wasn't right.

"Something's wrong," Henrie said. The army still hanged on Salosti's back. Finally he turned around angrily.

"I'm going home! Someone else can go play the hero's role; I quit!" As Salosti turned around again, he felt someone pulling his shoulders and forcing him to turn back. It was Dani.

"Salosti, you can't give up at this point! You didn't come this far to lose the game."

Salosti only pushed him away and said:

"I've already lost."

"That's it! It's no more Mr. nice guy! You're not quitting if it's gonna depend on me!" Dani shouted at Salosti shaking him viciously.

Salosti was shaking with anger too. Akii was yelling: "Stop fighting, you two!" Lumi was excited about the fight and was probably searching for a reason to join. Then King Henrie yelled: "STOP!" and everyone stopped.

Dani let go of Salosti, who headed for the cottage, and started to rub his dirty hands on his shirt. King Henrie spoke still facing the rest of the army.

"I'll talk to Salosti! I'm sure that I'll get him back. The rest of you, stay here! I'll be back in a minute."

The king walked into the cottage. There was not any furniture inside; only a shaggy bed on which Salosti lay. Somebody opened the door. The king walked beside the bed and Salosti rose to sit on the edge.

"What?" he asked, irritated that nobody would leave him alone.

"I wanna talk a bit. Firstly, what's happened?"

Salosti sighed: "Liisa's dead and I just..."

The king hushed him.

"What?" Salosti said edgily.

"I don't want you to tell the whole story. It only makes you feel worse. Now, what are you planning to do here?"

"Now I planned to just rest, and then go home."

The king thought for a moment.

"Well, Salosti, I think that you shouldn't return before it's done. I mean beating Raiwox, because if we don't do something quickly, we will end up being invaded by aliens or destroyed by Raiwox. You're the last hope, so please don't let us down after leading us so well this far."

Salosti thought for a moment, his thoughts somewhere else than this specific room.

"Once I beat Raiwox, will everything be happy; not only for the people but to me too? I mean, my life's been like an endless sacrifice. Every time I give up something and get something in return, it disappears. I never gain a reward that's permanent."

"I promise you'll end happily if you just don't give up," the king guaranteed. "But now I'm gonna leave you here to think these things we discussed about. By tomorrow I'm sure you have changed your mind."

The king walked away from the room, leaving Salosti alone. The young warrior started sleeping.

Salosti woke up late in the midnight. He heard some weird noises from outside. He pinched himself to check if he was only dreaming; it wasn't a dream. He decided to ignore the noises and drew his cover over his face.

Suddenly the window broke and Salosti heard gun sounds. Before he had noticed anything, there was a huge pain in his chest. A bullet had gone through his broken heart. He fell to the floor keeping his hands on his stomach. The hot blood was streaming down his body freely like a river. He couldn't fight against the pain anymore.

Our wounded hero found himself lying on the floor in the sea of his own blood. He saw a figure in his vision with his other eye that was still open. His mind was empty. He knew the figure in his vision, but couldn't remember who it was. Everything faded from his blur vision. He was dead...

Dani was sleeping in an abandoned building of Unhorimes. He woke up at midnight, hearing some weird sounds echoing in the empty building. He had been sleeping at the abandoned school with the army, but now he was in an unknown place all alone. Someone had apparently dragged him there. He got on his feet, scared. He looked around and lightened his wand. The noise came again, first from far away, but the echo made it come loud as if the person, or whatever it was, was nearer.

"Guys, it's not funny, I'm trying to sleep," Dani yelled, thinking it was just his friends pulling a prank. His voice echoed and came back as a scary whisper, then with plenty of other noises following it.

"Cut it out! I know it's you there! Come on out!" Dani was falling in the state of panic as he tried to convince himself that it was merely a prank. He heard the animal-like noises nearer and nearer. He didn't dare to yell anymore. The noises rebounded from the walls and were dancing inside his head. It was a torture. He was sweating and his heart was beating fast. He blocked his ears with his hands. Tears of despair filled his eyes.

Suddenly the noises were gone. Dani got on his feet relieved. Just then he heard an awful roar from behind him, and felt deadly pain in his stomach. He looked down and saw a blade of dripping blood sticking from his stomach. Someone had just impaled him with a sword. He felt how the assassin drew the sword back from his back while breathing heavily. Dani fell to the floor like a ragdoll. With the last ounces of his power he turned his head to see the assassin. It was King Henrie.

"You... why...?" he couldn't say more as he gave out his last breath. King Henrie, the traitor, had killed him.

End of Chapter VIII: Traitor

Chapter IX: The Dragon Rider

Salosti woke up in a foggy place, seeing nothing around him. He remembered now that it was King Henrie who had shot him. He didn't feel the pain anymore. "This must be heaven" he thought.

Even though the pain from his stomach was gone, his whole body felt angular. He moved his body parts that felt tired and robotic. His head hurt, like there was someone poking his brain. He felt sick.

Salosti put his hand on his chest and felt his heart beating; he wasn't dead. Regardless of that, he felt somehow empty and hollow. Something was missing once again. It wasn't Liisa, or Hajosiko or Kaste this time. It was something that had made his life worth living; the most important thing that he had possessed. And now it was gone. Salosti wondered what it could be.

The fog settled down and the tired leader found himself on a wooden floor. He got on his feet and looked around. He was in the cottage. There was no more his blood anywhere. "Was it a dream?" Salosti was absolutely confused. The only thing he remembered was King Henrie and a huge pain in his stomach. But now, the window was no more broken and the room was just like it had been when he had gone to sleep.

Salosti stretched. His muscles felt ruptured. It was as if he had just run twenty kilometers without stopping. He wasn't sure of anything anymore, except about that he was going crazy. He walked outside and headed to the town that was ruined after the battle. Many buildings were smoking after they had burned down. The streets were full of fallen men, guns and fissures. Salosti saw the abandoned school and walked in, being sure that his army would be there. He was right: Dani, Akii and Lumi were there. Salosti noticed that Henrie was missing. The leader was confused: "If he really killed me, why am I alive? And if he didn't, why is he gone now?"

"Hey, Salosti, you're back!" Lumi said happily. Akii examined Salosti with his gaze.

"Are you feeling good?" he asked. Salosti nodded even though it wasn't true. "You don't look so well." Salosti touched his forehead and it was hot.

Dani walked by Salosti and didn't seem as mad as he had been the other day.

"I found out who the traitor is: it's King Henrie."

Salosti watched away from Dani, thinking so hard that he could imagine his brain smoking like all the steam machines invented half-a-year ago.

"He killed me in my dream," Salosti said thoughtfully, "but how'd you know it's him, since nobody's murdered?"

"He impaled me with his sword at night... - WAIT! It's not possible, since I am alive right now! But... but I remember the pain when he sneaked from behind and stabbed the sword on my back! It felt so real... but was it a dream anyway?"

Salosti got excited. "Yeah, I remember the pain too! It couldn't have been a dream! And see; he's gone now! He wouldn't just stay after attempting to kill us and revealing himself."

Everybody was confused even though Dani and Salosti were the only ones that had dreamed about being killed by the same man.

"Maybe we're all in heaven," Lumi suggested.

"Or gone nuts," Akii said, "this is mysterious!"

Dani and Salosti were thinking for possible solutions to the strange incidence that seemed to not have anything that could explain the identical assassin-dreams and the mysterious disappearance of King Henrie.

"Maybe... NO, it can't be... but still... no, no... AAAH! This is @#$% CRAZY!!!" Dani yelled, since he didn't figure any explanations. Everybody laughed, even though Dani's aggression wasn't a joke; he only looked so funny when he was mad.

"Shut up! This is serious!" Dani yelled and everybody fell silent. Finally Akii came up with a plan.

"Why don't we just go to Mas Town, instead of just standing here? We have just one more tyrant to defeat then it's an open path to the Middle Island". The idea got positive feedback from the other boys, and so the army headed for Mas Town.

Before leaving Sir Wendell's Town, Salosti found Ferry and David, and warned them about the traitorous King Henrie's tergiversation. Ferry and David offered some of their men to join the remnants of Salosti's small army, but for some reason Salosti didn't want more people with him.

"You sure? It's gonna be the last tyrant, you know," Ferry reminded when hearing Salosti's response. Salosti didn't change his mind. He was proud of the remaining army that slew dozens of Kuoles and armored soldiers in a few seconds. The teamwork worked out perfectly and Salosti didn't want any of the lame royal knights to come spoil his army's tactics. He thought that they wouldn't learn how to work together with his people; it took time to learn to predict moves of enemies and allies and how to respond to them. Each person in Salosti's army had their personal strengths and weaknesses.

Akii was a great Supporter, helping Attackers by casting spells from the side, and healing hurt Defenders. Lumi was a middling Attacker, dashing ruthlessly, but sometimes effectively, to the masses of enemies. However his rushing often led him into a trouble, when he left the Supporters behind and got surrounded by enemies. Despite that recklessness, his aggressive methods proved to be a great way to push back the Kuoles.

Dani was an excellent Attacker, Supporter and Defender; he worked for all the duties and calmly thought before his actions. He cooperated well with Salosti. The leader himself was, like Dani, working at all the areas, because he thought that it was important for him to take responsibility of his own army.

Even though Salosti didn't get any backup from Ferry and David, he asked them to borrow him some money. The financial aid was more than enough; he got 500 golden coins. It was a big money!

When Salosti returned to his army, he raised the money pouch high above his head so that everybody saw it.

"Gentlemen, tonight we're gonna sleep in a hotel!" Everybody cheered and went up the hill where their stolen flycycles lay rusty. Lumi's fuel was low, so he used the flycycle that King Henrie had used.

Everybody joked around and was happy during the traveling. Salosti felt much more comfortable than he had before the Battle for Unhorimes. His hope and desires were back. His homesickness wasn't so bad anymore. However, he still felt empty inside like he had in the morning, and he wondered what it was about.

Salosti and his army were resting in a five-star hotel room. Salosti rubbed his calf that had cramped during the cycling. His body still felt very weird and tired.

"I think my body's starting to collapse. We haven't practiced for ages, and now my muscles feel stiff," he said thoughtfully.

"Aww, Salosti, don't be depressing. Relax a little," Dani said cheerfully. A headwaiter walked inside the room holding a huge server full of all kinds of elegant food. Everybody but Salosti rushed around the table on which the headwaiter placed the server. The leader stood on his spot and scratched his head.

Akii pointed at the seat beside him: "Join in, Salosti! Quickly before Lumi eats everything but the table" he said. Dani laughed.

Salosti still stood on his spot. "Um, I'm gonna wash my hands first," he said and entered the enormous bathroom. He washed his hands and stared at his reflection in the mirror. His skin was dirty and full of scars and scratches. His hair was long and messy. His teeth weren't in a good shape either.

The young man was shocked about how badly he had maintained his hygiene. He decided to take a shower. He took off his armor and other clothes and smelled them. They smelled like a mixture of blood, sand, grass, sweat and rust. He decided to wash his armor and clothes as well as taking the shower, then to sharpen his sword and practice his magic.

After Salosti had taken a shower and washed his armor and clothes, he felt refreshed. He hung his armor on a pipe to dry and put on his clothes. Then he walked back to the room. Dani and

Lumi were sleeping, their stomachs full. Akii was still eating. Salosti knew that he had delayed, because he wanted to talk with him.

Salosti walked to the table and sat opposite to Akii. There was still some food left. Akii smiled.

"You're lucky that I concealed your portion" he said and glanced at the sleeping Lumi. Salosti laughed and sighed.

"Aah, I feel reborn! You guys should wash yourself and your stuff likewise".

Akii examined Salosti with his stare.

"Wow! I didn't remember that you were THAT light-skinned," he laughed "Now you sure are a 'Warrior of Light'! Geez, it almost hurts my eyes!"

Salosti had forgotten how fun it was with Akii, since the boy had been so loyal to King Henrie, and the two had not had much time to spend together during the quest. Salosti finished his meal and went to lie down on a sofa. He fell asleep immediately. Akii yawned, wiped his eyes tiredly and went to sleep as well.

Salosti found himself in a foggy place. "AGAIN!?" he said aloud. He pinched himself. It didn't hurt; it was just a dream. He saw clouds all around him. Soon eight figures appeared in his vision, dancing in the distance, yelling his name. Salosti recognized most of them. Hajosiko, Liisa and Kaste were there waving their arms and cheering. Salosti ran by them. Liisa ran by his arms and kissed him on the cheek. All the others surrounded him, hugging, squeezing, patting and shaking him. Salosti knew he was in heaven, but didn't know why. Nor did he care. He was crying for happiness about seeing all his lost friends again.

"What's this place, guys?" Salosti asked tears streaming down his face. He couldn't feel it physically, only inside.

His question wasn't answered directly.

"Please tell me that you saved Earth before dying," Liisa begged.

"Dying? I don't remember anything like that… except… but it was a dream…" Salosti tried to make sense of things. His friends were puzzled.

"I… I'm confused. I'm sorry but I guess that Raiwox isn't dead yet," Salosti admitted sadly. A stranger walked by Salosti and said;

"I think Salosti's not dead yet either". Everybody gasped.

"Wh… what'd you mean? Who are you?" Salosti asked the man that seemed noble by his clothing and the way he spoke.

"Why, I am the soul of Wanhaz," said the man. The man continued, "I found a way to replicate myself so that I could continue my research even after my death. As I died by accident when one of my inventions blew up, my rotten side was released, Raiwox. Instead of being an identical copy of me, he ended up being the combination of all my bad traits doubled. I'm the real Wanhaz, the scientist from WOP who researched the unknown, and the man who wreaks havoc in your world is the result of my experiment."

Salosti bowed humbly to Wanhaz's real being. "Sir, I promise I will defeat your clone if I get another chance." Wanhaz patted Salosti's and replied "Good boy!"

Salosti straightened himself up again and begged "Could you now explain me what you meant by "I'm not dead", sir." Wanhaz seemed pleased for Salosti's royal treatment.

"I think that if you aren't dead, but you're still here, it means that you have only lost your soul."

"My soul?! How's that even possible?"

The old man explained calmly. "Son, some people, like you and I, have the ability to see through the eyes of their soul. That means that if your soul, like it is, is in heavens, you can come here every time you close your eyes in mortal world."

"So, I can go back if I just open my eyes and awake from my dream?" Salosti asked.

"Yes, son. It's that easy."

Salosti looked down sorrowfully. "Damn, I never knew how much the soul is worth!"

The leader of the Warriors turned to face his friends. He talked a lot with them about how the things were going down on Earth. Salosti was so happy; he could now be with his friends anytime he wanted, even though they were physically dead. It still felt so unreal that he was afraid that it would turn out to be just a dream.

Finally he decided to wake up, because he had a lot to do with his army. He waved his hand and the vision vanished from his sight.

In the morning, everybody but Salosti washed themselves and their clothes. They were all amazed about the result of a single shower. Everybody almost "shined" after all the dirt was gone. The boys had been accustomed to the smell of sweat, during the days of army life, so they didn't notice it was gone. But they noticed when it was back.

Salosti paid to the owner of the hotel and the group left the hotel and continued traveling with their flycycles.

Finally the four reached the infamous Mas Town. They didn't have troubles about finding the king's castle. It was an enormous, dark tower in the middle of the town. Salosti was nervous when walking towards the tower. He tried to imagine the third tyrant and the powers he possessed.

While walking through the town, Dani, Salosti, Wanhaz, Akii and Lumi saw how cruel-looking most of the people were. Tax ghosts were everywhere and Salosti had to stop to pay for one. The whole army was anxious.

"Raiwox is getting intense" Lumi whispered as he saw how a poor man was executed by a Tax Ghost for not paying.

"Oh, you noticed!" Dani replied sarcastically.

The five reached the dark tower. They opened the door with a spell, and rushed in. They saw only circular stairs that led upwards. It was the only direction where to go.

The stairs seemed endless and everybody's feet were getting tired. Finally, though, the stairs led to a platform. There were no walls surrounding the roof. Salosti could see the whole town as a bunch of dots in the background. Besides the town, he saw a foggy forest in the south, and a crystalline sparkling clear lake from which some antelopes were drinking, in the north.

It was a beautiful view. Salosti almost fell into his fantasies as usual, but then he remembered why he was there in the first place. He looked around the platform and found an unknown, black coated man, his back facing the army. The man turned around. A hood that was drawn over his head blocked his face.

Lumi dashed ruthlessly towards the man from the side and struck him with his sword. The man grunted and made a sneaky counterattack: he waited until Lumi was about to hit again, then cast a spell from under his coat. The spell first thrust Lumi so that he fell down, then made the platform shake as if it was an earthquake.

"Get down and grab onto something!" Salosti yelled over the quaking noises. He himself stabbed his sword on the platform and held tight on it. With the corner of his eye he saw the tyrant jumping from the platform. He gasped, but then saw the tyrant rising from beneath on the back of a black, scaly dragon.

The dragon hit Lumi with its tail, causing the cantankerous warrior to fly three meters upwards. Lumi didn't land on the platform anymore; he had fallen down into the city. Salosti heard Dani and Akii casting spells on the vigorous dragon. The leader took his sword from the platform and jumped on the dragon's tail before it flew farther from the tower.

Now the creature headed away from the tower. Salosti screamed and hanged on the dragon's tail that was swinging violently. The hero stabbed his sword on the dragon's tail like he had done to the platform for better grip. As he did that, green, fluctuate liquid spurted to his face. He couldn't see for a while.

At the same time, Akii ran down the circular stairs in hopes of getting some help from the citizens. Finally he reached the bottom of the tower and rushed to the mayor's house to tell about the dragon above the town.

Salosti had finally gotten to a better position on the dragon's back. The tyrant was sitting six meters from him on the dragon's neck. The dragon was breathing fire and destroying the town.

"Attention, warriors of light! If you don't surrender, my dragon will destroy not only the people of this town, but also your dear friend up here!" the dragon rider announced with a loud, scary voice. Salosti was shocked to hear that the tyrant had noticed him.

The dragon rider guided his pet to crush its tail into buildings to get rid of the freeloader. Salosti dodged and protected himself for his life.

Suddenly the dark sky was full of searchlights trying to point at the dragon. The panzers raised their pipes towards the sky.

"No, no! We didn't want this kind of help! You're gonna kill my friend if you shoot it down!" Akii tried to explain to the mayor who didn't listen. The panzers aimed and fired. The first shots missed. But they aimed the second ones and…

Salosti had climbed his way to the dragon's back. He dashed towards the dragon rider, who was trying to cast spells on Salosti and control the dragon at the same time. One of his spells hit Salosti in the face. It was an unknown darkness-spell to him. It made his vision blur and balance weak. It was just the spell for that specific situation.

Salosti still kept his balance and reached the dragon rider and hit him in the face. The evil one lost the control of the dragon, and it crashed through a building that collapsed afterwards. The winged horror's wings were now critically gashed and its flying became unstable. Salosti still couldn't see well for the darkness-spell.

"You wounded my darling! I will kill you, you little brat!" the dragon rider shouted into Salosti's ear.

The warrior felt how the tyrant grabbed his face and cast a strong aero-spell. Salosti flew through the air and crashed on a building. He lost his consciousness and started falling towards the ground at a high speed.

"NO!" Akii yelled pointing at the sky. Luckily his friend fell on a soft marketplace. Akii poured water on his face, and Salosti woke up.

"Where… how… is he dead?" he said fuzzily.

Akii pointed to the sky where the wounded dragon flew aimlessly, wounded. Finally one of the panzers shot it down. Its rider fell first, twenty meters and hit the ground breaking all his bones.

The dragon was falling slowly, bleeding the green stuff that rained to the town. After a while, it fell roughly to the ground and landed just where its rider had. Both were dead.

The citizens cheered, not for the warriors, but for the military. Salosti and Akii didn't even want to celebrate now.

"Where're Dani and Lumi?" Salosti asked. Just then Dani and Lumi arrived, the former leading and supporting the other boy's wounded body.

"He fell from the tower, and I saved him" Dani explained. Then he talked to Lumi playfully "Well, what do nice people say when they get rescued, hmm?"

"Thank… you…" Lumi said with a weak voice. This was the first time Salosti had heard him thanking about anything.

"Well are we celebrating, or what?" Dani asked.

"Are you kidding? We're now ready to get Raiwox and you wanna celebrate?" Salosti said. "He is getting angrier all the time, so we don't have time for tea parties".

"Who says it has to be a teaparty? It can be a slumber party!" Lumi said stupidly. Salosti, Akii and Dani looked at each other, thinking about the same thing, and sighed.

End of Chapter IX: The Dragon Rider

Chapter X: Dominion of the Evil

Valo had now arrived on Earth to accompany Wuol. They had given up searching for Wanhaz, but they wondered where Tainelm could be.

"We can't escape from this world anymore; we're doomed to live on this war-planet," Valo said gloomily after asking around about the progress of the battle.

"What do you mean?" Wuol inquired.

"I've heard that the Warriors of Light have created a magical shield called 'Black Curtain', around this planet to prevent the rest of our armored soldiers from coming. But that shield also prevents us from leaving this place. Maybe we better fight our way out of this."

Wuol shook her head.

"We're not taking any sides in this idiotic bedevilment. We didn't want this. It was the Mayor of the first floor who encouraged our people to fight for an invasion over a new world. But we're not taking part of their lunacy. We'll be wise and escape."

Valo nodded. It wasn't their fault that there was a war of three different races on Earth. "I'll escape with you," he said, "We'll find a peaceful place that we can call home. Let's go!"

The two went on a journey to find a spot without the horrific scenes of war.

Salosti and the others were resting in an inn. They weren't wasting their money for expensive hotels anymore, even though they had money to spare. Salosti remembered his dream last night about the heaven. He decided to sleep again to see if it had been just a realistic dream, or was it really true that he had lost his soul and could go to heaven whenever he closed his eyes.

Shutting his eyelids, the hero found himself in the same cloudy place again with all his friends there. He heard their voices, but his vision was blurry.

"You're back!" Everybody yelled excitedly. Salosti didn't feel their touches anymore. Something was wrong. "I can't see or feel anymore," he said hopelessly.

He heard how the wise Wanhaz walked by him.

"I think I can explain you," he said. Salosti raised his head. "Raiwox must have found a way to blind the eyes of your soul," he explained. "He knows that as long as you can see us, you have hope. Thus he blinded your vision in here. He obviously wants you to fall into deep despair and lose your hope when you can't see us anymore."

All Salosti saw was white and some faint, foggy figures. He shook his head.

"Well if he thinks he can break me down, he's wrong! Because I'm not letting this kind of trick break my spirit. I may be blind here, but just knowing that you're really here, and hearing your voices is enough to keep me going."

"Good boy!"

Salosti couldn't see his friends clearly, so he didn't find a reason to be in heavens anymore. He saw Liisa's faint face the most clearly for some reason. He turned to her and said: "I'll be back soon!" Liisa wanted to embrace Salosti, but he turned around and prepared to return to Earth before she had a chance.

Hajosiko immediately took the chance when Salosti had gone away. He walked by Liisa when Kaste wasn't seeing. While flying through the clouds towards the earth surface to return his body, Salosti turned his head to wave goodbye to his friends, and saw what Hajosiko was doing: that bastard was embracing Liisa, who was crying, because he was gone again, and would probably never see them again since Raiwox had messed up his vision in heavens. Salosti wanted to kill Hajosiko right that moment, taking advantage of his absence and the girl's fragile state. But then he woke up back in the inn.

Salosti got up in the dark room and saw everybody else sleeping. He was tired but didn't dare to go back to heaven. He walked to the bathroom and hanged his sweaty armor to dry. He looked at the mirror and yelled aloud:

"I hate him!"

Suddenly Lumi came in rubbing his tired eyes.

"What were you yelling about?" He asked yawning.

"Nothing… uh, the people in that other room kept a loud noise, so I…"

"Whatever! Just let us sleep!" Lumi walked back to the other room and lay down on a sofa. He started snoring immediately.

Salosti still didn't want to sleep and go back to heaven. He was so mad at Hajosiko right that moment that he didn't want to see him anytime soon.

Our hero waited until his friends had awakened. Then he, Dani, Akii, and Lumi walked down the wooden stairs. Salosti paid for the owner of the inn, and they left.

"What are we gonna do now?" Lumi asked when the army was outside.

"We've got to find that damned King Henrie, so we can return him to his throne to open path to the Middle Island," Dani replied, "But capturing him might be difficult, considering the fact that he's the traitor who's siding with Raiwox now."

"But why was he captured and imprisoned in the Underworld if he was supporting the tyrants?" Akii wondered aloud.

The four were walking on a long road in a grassy place. They stopped in their tracks when they saw a magical letter floating towards them. Akii picked it up and read who it was addressed for. Then he gave it to Salosti. It was from Ferry and David.

Hey, Salosti

We've got some good news and we've got some bad news.

Good news first:

We have rescued the two original kings and returned them

to their thrones. Now we only need to find Henrie and bring him

to the kingdom of Dalik Islands.

Also, even though the aliens lost the Battle for Unhorimes,

they're gonna send their troops here (they have plenty of people).

However, we connected the powers of the two original kings

and made a shield called the "Black Curtain", surrounding Earth.

It prevents most of the aliens from coming here.

Now for the bad news:

Aliens and Kuoles seem to have connected their powers to take us down.

They're trying to destroy the spell of the "Black Curtain"

which is in a guarded secret bunker. If they succeed, we'll be in trouble.

The leader of the Kuoles and armored soldiers is a gigantic robot general called

Caispea, who works for Raiwox as a war leader.

They also have two other leaders called Tainelm and the "Commander".

Salosti finished the letter. Their fears had come true: Kuoles and aliens had teamed up against the Last Warriors of Light!

"Geez, can't those two do anything without our help," Salosti said, being disappointed to Ferry and David for the first time. It wasn't fair that they had to go somewhere to aid two other armies just when they could go fight Raiwox himself. However, his sense of justice prevented him from refusing to help his comrades in distress. He turned to face the three other Warriors.

"We've gotta go to Snow Isles. The bunker is there."

Lumi moaned like always:

"No! Not Snow Isles again! It's cold there!"

"Shut up, princess!" Salosti said, infuriated. Dani and Akii looked at each other and burst into laugh:

"Pft aha ha ha haa!" Their laugh caught Salosti too. Coming to think of it, the word "princess" fit Lumi perfectly; always complaining like a spoiled brat.

"Stop mocking me, or I'm going to quit!" Lumi shouted.

Salosti wiped his eyes, still smiling.

"Sorry! Just joking," he said. Lumi made an "okay then" look.

The four went on a journey to the Snow Isles.

On the way to Snow Isles the army heard news about Caispea and his armies of Kuoles and armored soldiers (or aliens as most earthlings called them). They destroyed towns, villages and cities. The robot general's army took over the conquered places and enslaved the overtaken citizens like Ferry and David had told. Caispea had taken dominion of the whole Earth; Raiwox's plan had really succeeded.

Finally Salosti, Akii, Dani, and Lumi reached Snow Isles. They made a camp with their brand new camping set, near to the bunker. Salosti received message from David and Ferry in which they told his army not to come till they received a sign that the base was under attack. Otherwise, they just needed to be on watch, and if any intruders tried to break in, they needed to be eliminated. Salosti's army was prepared for anything. They all were in good shape, except they were out of money again.

"I'm hungry," Lumi whined.

"Go get some food from the town," Salosti said absently staring at the fire.

"But we've got no money," Akii reminded.

"No matter, remember...?"

"Oh, yeah: It's for good! We're saving Earth, so it's not bad if we commit some minimal crimes," Lumi said getting excited "The end justifies the means, huh? Who's coming with me?"

"Me!" Dani and Akii yelled at the same time. They went.

"Get something for me too!" Salosti yelled after them. He knew that stealing food wasn't a good thing, but something had made him neglectful about what was good and what was bad. He decided to visit the heavens through his soul again, because he wanted some answers from the wise Wanhaz.

Salosti was in the cloudy place again. He still couldn't see well for Raiwox's spell or whatever trick it was. He heard the others come around him, everybody talking at the same time. Salosti didn't even have time to open his mouth when he felt his soul returning back to his body. "Someone must've awakened me," he thought, because he had the power to control his time in heavens, except if he woke up.

He woke up by the fire, Dani shaking his body.

"You can't sleep when there can be enemies and you're all alone!" he said seriously. Then he turned more casual, "Look what we got! Ta-dah! Oven heated pizza for everyone! Here this is yours," he handed a hot, fumy pizza to confused Salosti who took it and started eating. All the others ate as well. Besides the pizzas, they had stolen plenty of other food that seemed to be enough for two weeks.

Just as Salosti, Dani, Akii and Lumi had mostly finished eating, they saw a huge object flying above them. The object seemed like an airplane, except much, much bigger. The shadow that it cast covered the whole snowy forest. It took it about ten seconds for it to cross the forest. It was flying towards the town.

"What the heck?" Lumi exclaimed, his mouth full of pizza. Akii choked to his slice and Salosti went to pat his back. Dani only stood frozen, his mouth open wide.

"I think it was Caispea," he whispered, "He's gonna take over the town and enslave the people! We must stop him!"

The army dashed down the steep, slippery hill. They fell many times, but continued going relentlessly. They soon had reached the town. Dani had been right; it was Caispea. He stood on a roof of a church. The cleric who had been holding a synagogue inside, ran outside, followed by the church parish. The shopkeepers ran outside as well from their businesses, and headed for the church. Now the sacred place was surrounded by all the people of the town.

Caispea spoke with a sinister, robotic voice.

"Citizens, I have come to take over this town to expand my realms that I willingly impart to my creator's, Raiwox's, kingdom," he made an effective pause and looked around to see how his listeners would react. "As you people may already know, Raiwox isn't the kind of man who doesn't care about the people. He is merciful to you as long as you don't disobey his simple rules," he made a pause again. "If you people let us take this town to our use, we'll be pleased and don't have to fight you. If you resist, however, you can say goodbye to your lives. So, which will it be?"

The mayor of the town stepped forward. He cleared his throat nervously.

"I believe that there is no need for a battle," he said.

Caispea was pleased. "Good, now if nobody defies us, we'll do it the easy way... - Shackle them!" he yelled and a wicket from his belly opened. Armored soldiers and Kuoles came out and jumped to the town. They held chains that would connect the slaves to each other, and were armed despite the fact that no one dared to fight back.

Salosti and the others were frozen for a second. Then they withdrew their weapons and started fighting. Salosti battled near Lumi and Dani, but Akii was nowhere to be seen. The leader of the Warriors started to get worried. Their teamwork wouldn't work perfectly unless Akii was helping. Suddenly there came a loud roar from the direction of Caispea. Salosti raised his head and saw Akii on the roof of the church, fighting the robot.

Akii dodged Caispea's hands that went through the roof of the church. Then he jumped on the robot's face and cast a water-spell. The shock wave made the robot roar in pain again. He shook his head so that Akii fell back on the roof. The robot picked up the cross from the roof and charged an attack on Akii, who didn't have time to dodge.

Salosti gasped, as his friend was slashed with a sharp metal cross. Blood was splattered as the boy fell from the roof to the other side of the building. Salosti ran for the church. The drop had been at least five meters and the landing was not soft.

Caispea and his infamous army had taken control of the town already. Salosti went around the ruined church and found his best friend lying on a thorny bush. He had a serious-looking gash in his stomach, and his eyes were staring blindly in his head.

"Salosti... you can do it without me... I didn't choose you for nothing... right? My Order was to choose you. In the future, the mankind will live happily because I made the right choice. And this is only a small price to pay for what will come. 'The end justifies the means', right?"

"Stop talking like that," Salosti begged, "You're not gonna die, you'll be alright."

"Please, save this fallen world... I'll say hi to Liisa, Hajosiko and Kaste for you..."

Akii shut his eyes slowly and stopped moving. Salosti started crying uncontrollably. This was truly an endless nightmare. Why could it not end? Salosti dragged his friend to the snowy forest outside the town. He still couldn't believe it all. This was not happening! All of his childhood friends were now gone...

In the forest he started to cast healing spells on Akii's body. The gashes healed well so that only few scars were left. However, Akii still didn't move. Salosti sighed depressed. For some reason the deaths of other people weren't so shocking anymore. He thought that he was so accustomed to them, and hated himself for it. He could not cry as much as he wanted to. The army life had made him cold and unemotional.

"So long, friend," Salosti said aloud. He surprised himself with the calmness of his voice. "You could have chosen someone else... someone who could have saved you too."

The snow of the blizzard covered Akii's body. Salosti took his own sword and put it on the snow as a memoriam for his brave friend. *He had his complete trust in me, and I let him die,* Salosti thought sorrowfully. He walked back to the town to search for Dani and Lumi. He had to avoid the Kuoles and aliens so that he would not get captured and enslaved like all the other citizens were now; they had lost the battle within minutes. An armored soldier with a robe and a crown was giving orders to his minions. Salosti guessed that he was the "Commander" that Ferry and David had mentioned in the letter.

Since Salosti didn't find Dani or Lumi in the chains, he decided to return to the camp. Dani was sitting there full of scratches after the battle. He seemed happy to see Salosti. Lumi, however, was not there.

"I knew you couldn't die! Where's Akii?" Dani asked.

"Dead," Salosti replied and sat down on a log. "How about Lumi? Where's he?"

"He escaped. Told me that he missed his family like Liisa had back then. I knew he was lying; during these days if there's something I've learned about Lumi, it is that he simply cannot love. I guess the real reason why he left was the fear of Raiwox's wrath... Poor coward! But in a way I'm happy that he's gone."

"I hate him too. I hated him since the first time I met him," Salosti admitted. Dani nodded in comprehension.

"So, I guess it's just you and I from now on," he continued, sighing.

"Yeah!" Dani replied. "You know, since we formed this army, we've lost soldiers one by one... Most of them have died, one was a traitor, and one escaped. Maybe Raiwox has cursed us with black magic, or something."

"I don't care if he has. We won't lose; I promised to my friends," Salosti said.

"Yeah, as long as we two stay together this army will never be terminated," Dani agreed.

The two went to their sleeping bags and started sleeping. Salosti thought that his vision in heaven would still be foggy, but this time he didn't see anything at all except for infinite darkness as he closed his eyes.

"I can't see anything! Are you guys there," he tried to call the other souls, but didn't hear a response. "Has Raiwox taken my whole soul away from heaven?" he thought. He saw simply nothing in his dream until he woke up. "But how can he know what I am doing?"

He lay on the ground without getting any sleep. He was thinking about what his Order would tell him to do, and when he would hear it. Once again, his head was full of unsolved mysteries.

Meanwhile, when Wuol and Valo were crossing a town occupied by armored soldiers and Kuoles, they ran to their old friend, Tainelm, who was leading the troops and giving orders. Wuol and Valo were happy to see their old friend again.

"Oh, it's you, friends!" Tainelm smiled, obviously dissimulating his emotions. As a war leader, he seemed to be very busy, and seemed to have forgotten about everything else.

"We are gonna live in some place peaceful without any lunacy such as this absurd war, going on. We'd be happy if you'd join us!" Valo said. Tainelm seemed apathetic.

"But we're so close to victory in this new world. The inhabitants are tough, but we can beat them very soon if we just find a way to remove the Black Curtain. Then we'd just send the rest of our people here. We'd outnumber them so that they couldn't stand a chance against us."

Wuol and Valo were worried. They were sure that the power over an army and taking over nations had messed up Tainelm's mind; they were partially right.

One of the armored soldiers walked by Tainelm and gave him a letter. He read it and seemed pleased.

"Excellent! The Commander is going to get rid of the remaining two warriors. If it doesn't work, Caispea will be the one to do it! After that we have already won!"

He turned to face the two friends of his and smiled happily.

"Once this is done, I'll go with you guys! Then we'll all live happily together."

He walked away. Wuol and Valo looked at each other. "What happened to the way he used to speak?"

Tainelm talked to the Mayor, showing him some war-plans, and the two neutrals walked away.

Salosti was still awake in the midnight. He got up and saw that Dani wasn't in his sleeping bag anymore. The hero was sure that the other boy was just practicing or doing something else that was surely harmless. He had learned to trust Dani almost as much as he had trusted Akii. When thinking about Akii, Salosti, for some reason, felt a need to visit the grave one last time, as if to check that he was really resting in peace. He didn't even know why, but he walked through the forest until he found the sword sticking on the snow. He walked by the grave.

Suddenly he heard a voice from behind him. He withdrew his sword out of reflex and turned around. It was Dani.

"What the heck are you sneaking about in the midnight?" Salosti questioned.

"I could ask you the same," Dani replied, "But we don't have time for explanations. Come on, follow me!" Dani turned around and headed for the heart of the forest. Salosti followed him in confusion.

Finally Dani stopped and pointed at a weird, metallic machine standing in the empty place. Black electric waves seemed to generate energy in the machine. The engine was a dome over a crystalline dust.

"This is a time machine," Dani explained, "I used the crystal dust, even though it's illegal, to build this. I thought that you may want to go back in time and save our army, and perhaps somehow, stop the coming of aliens. Then we would all be together and have better chances in beating Raiwox, without having to worry about the invaders. And best of all, none of us needs to die. You see, as things are now, the probability of us two winning is very low…"

Salosti nodded thinking "Now I can save Liisa… And this time I'll know from the start who the traitor is, so I'll have the advantage."

Finally the leader made up his mind.

"Send us to the day we reached Snow Town. There Kaste died; it was the first death of a Warrior. Since that day our army's been shrinking. This time we'll make sure nobody dies!"

"Roger that!" Dani said and led Salosti to the machine.

"Ready?" He said and pushed a button.

A huge explosion followed. Salosti felt how his body burst on flames. He heard Dani screaming. Salosti himself flew five meters away from the machine and landed roughly on the ice. The project had obviously failed.

With the last ounces of his power, Salosti raised his head to see if Dani had survived. He saw nothing but fire and smoke all around. For his relief, he finally saw his wounded comrade squirming from the fire saying something like "…this is sabotage". Looking closely, Salosti saw that the other boy's legs were missing. Salosti saw that there were line wires sticking from Dani's broken body parts. Salosti took a look at his own hands. Another arm was broken, some cables sticking from it as well. But he did not feel any pain, nor was there any blood.

"We're… we're robots!" Salosti exclaimed. He heard a maniacal laughter and raised his head to see an armored soldier with a crown and a cloak.

"The Commander!' Salosti said aloud. The Commander removed his mask and Salosti saw King Henrie's face, black rings around his darkly blinded eyes. He laughed the horrific maniac laughter again.

"YOU!" Dani and Salosti exclaimed at the same time.

End of Chapter X: Dominion of the Evil

Chapter XI: Destiny

Salosti got on his feet painfully and dashed towards the king while drawing out his sword with his unbroken arm. He was confused about everything, but his strongest emotion right that moment was anger. He charged at the "Commander's" neck with his sword. The slash cut off Henrie's head that flew through the air, far away. Only his headless body remained, blood spluttering from his neck. Salosti regretted his actions immediately; they still were supposed to return Henrie to his throne. But now he was dead. The warrior heard a voice and raised his head. He saw a young man who looked slightly like Dani. The stranger was holding a video-camera, standing on a boulder. He laughed sinisterly.

"Well, well, if isn't the leader of the Last Warriors killing their beloved king," he said. Salosti understood that the stranger had just filmed the whole killing scene.

"Who are you? Why are you filming me?" Salosti asked. He could tell the other man was not from Earth as such technology had been banned there.

"I'm Tainelm, the leader of the armored soldiers. Raiwox, our ally, telepathically hypnotized King Henrie to terminate your army. I came here with my people to get a new home. We were just some rats in our rotten sandbox, but now we're something much more as we are soon the new ruling race of earth."

Salosti had difficulties to understand Tainelm's pronunciation.

"I understand you," he said honestly, "You wanted to get away from your old home to find some place new. I did the same thing; I escaped when I got bored of my old life. We're alike. So, why would you wanna side with the bad guys? You people could have just come to live with us peacefully."

Tainelm got Salosti's point, but didn't want to admit it.

"I'm going to show this video to the losers who still believe in the Last Warriors. You're going to lose this war no matter what! I've got an evidence of your tergiversation. Once the truth will be revealed, the WOP will get the land that they deserve!"

Tainelm turned around and started running away with the camera in his tight grip. Salosti tried to catch him, but the other man outran him easily since Salosti was seriously injured. He fell on his knees and looked at his machine arms and legs. *No wonder I've been feeling so weird lately...*

"This must be a dream! This can't be happening..."

Dani walked beside him and patted his shoulder.

"It's okay. We may have lost the citizens from our side with that cowardly trick, but we still have Ferry and David besides each other."

Salosti looked at his body again and saw metallic parts here and there.

"Why are we robots? Have we always been?"

Dani looked at his metallic legs that he had just fixed with a spell.

"I suppose this has something to do with our dreams about being killed by Henrie. Maybe we really died and our hearts and brains were put into these armors."

"But why?" Salosti asked.

Dani only shook his head. "I don't know. Let's return to the camp."

The two left the burning forest and dragged Henrie's dead body with them: dead or not, he had to be returned to his throne.

Salosti didn't get any sleep. He didn't even want to because he knew he wouldn't see anything. Many things were confusing him like why he was a robot all of a sudden. The mysteries seemed endless and he wondered if he could ever solve them all. Luckily Dani had fixed his arm and other wounds. Salosti thought about the first day when he had left his home. He knew that he had learned a lot since that day. But still he thought that he wasn't the right boy for the quest to beat Raiwox. He didn't even dare to imagine how powerful the final tyrant could be. *I understand why Lumi left... I am afraid too.*

All of a sudden Salosti rose up and started walking automatically without the will of his own. It was like someone else was controlling him. He couldn't yell for help or fight back the forceful movement of his body. He knew this had something to do with him being a robot. He wished that Dani would wake up.

"Has Raiwox or someone else taken over my body?" Salosti thought in panic. "Is this magic or technology?"

He now saw the bunker in which the spell of the Black Curtain was kept. There were soldiers from armies of Ferry and David on guard. Salosti simply marched through the masses, slaying the soldiers with his sword on the way. He went inside and walked through many rooms until he reached a room in which the glowing spell of the Black Curtain was floating under a dome. All the guards in there were taken down easily. The hero tried in vain to stop himself from killing his own allies.

Salosti's body walked to the dome and lifted it off. Just then he heard a yell from behind him.

"Salosti, how could you fall to their side?"

His head turned and he saw Dani first at the door, then rushing towards him, then holding his throat and hitting him in the face repeatedly. Salosti laid on the ground, helplessly, his friend trying to kill him.

"I thought that I could trust you!" Dani yelled hitting harder each time and almost crying at the same time. Salosti felt how something broke from his neck. It was not a part of his body. Now he was able to control his body again.

"Stop! Please! I can explain…" he wheezed, but Dani didn't listen. Salosti was sure that he was going to die soon. But then came a loud crash that interrupted his comrade's wrath. The wall beside him broke and something came in. Both, Salosti and Dani, turned to see who it was. It was Caispea. The two gasped and Dani released Salosti from his grip.

Caispea roared at Dani:

"Just when our plan was about to work you meddling brat come to ruin everything!"

"What are you talking about?" Dani asked confused.

"You two may have been feeling a bit empty lately. Well that's because the Commander killed you and we build robot versions of you by using your hearts, brains and flesh. We were hoping that we could've controlled you to use in our armies. Think about that; the two greatest Warriors on our side. It would make our victory confident. But just when the "control stick" we installed on Salosti's neck started to function and we were in full control of him, you came and broke it by hitting him in the head. Now we can't control him anymore."

"What about my "control stick"?" Dani asked and tried to find something in the back of his neck with his fingers.

"For some reason it didn't work. Therefore we planned to use Salosti to terminate you. At any rate, it seems like I must destroy the spell of the Black Curtain by myself, since I finally found it! But first I'm gonna get rid of you two. After that we've won already! Mu ha ha haaa!"

Salosti broke in. "You're wrong! Even if you beat us, there's still Ferry and David and their armies!"

The robot laughed with mockery.

"What's so funny?"

"You idiots! Haven't you noticed that mostly everything around you is only an illusion? Ferry and David are on OUR side; didn't you notice how many times they delayed your mission with calls for help? They only pretend to be on your side, but were Raiwox's servants all along. They led the two armies to a trap where Akii's Warriors were killed and turned into Kuoles and Tax Ghosts after the show that was Batlle for Unhorimes."

"But we can't die, since it's Salosti's Destiny to beat Raiwox! We've followed all the Orders and..." Dani said. Once again Caispea laughed, interrupting him.

"Those are illusions too! Orders are just illusions created by Raiwox to gather potential threats together and destroy them all at once. The Destiny you speak of is just as big of a lie. The only common destiny for everyone is death! You've been fooled by illusions!"

Once Salosti and Dani heard that the Orders and Destiny weren't real, their spirit vanished. They knew now that all they had was each other against the rest of the world. And their victory was not certain at all, for their Destiny was not written in stars, and they themselves were the only ones who controlled what was to happen. Both withdrew their weapons depressed and prepared to fight their final fight.

Caispea's hands turned into drills, and guns were sticking out from the holes in his body parts. Salosti and Dani were a great team even though they felt they couldn't stand a chance. They combined their attacks, doing damage from multiple directions at once, all the while protecting and supporting one another. Soon the robot general's right arm exploded and fell off of his body in flames. He roared with amok.

"My arm!" Then he turned overly confident again. "Heh, no matter! You two will die anyway very soon! There's absolutely no way you're getting away with this!"

Caispea jumped through the ceiling and flew away.

Both, Salosti and Dani were silent for a moment. They tried to lift the dome off to get the spell to a safe hidden place, but it protected itself by casting spells on the two anytime they went near the dome.

"I guess we've got to count on its defense system, because we can't take it with us," Dani said after several tries. Salosti agreed. "But it may well be so that the Black Curtain, too, is merely an illusion that Ferry and David used to make us believe that they are on our side, and that we had to travel here instead of going to face Raiwox."

Salosti nodded again. He didn't feel like talking. Suddenly Dani gasped and yelled:

"What the heck is that you got there?" He pointed at Salosti's belly. The leader looked down and saw some kind of digital horologe with time 14:09:98 that was running one second at a time. The numbers became smaller and smaller each second. On the top there was a big number 17. Dani had an identical "clock" with Salosti in his belly, except it wasn't running.

"I think it's a time bomb!" Salosti exclaimed shocked. Dani gasped. "See?" Salosti continued. "That big 17 represents the days, and these are hours and minutes!"

Dani started to panic.

"We've got to stop that timer or you'll explode after 16 days and 14 hours! Quickly, help me take it off!"

The two tried several times, but didn't get the time bomb off, nor could they stop it. They wondered why their enemies had given them so much time before the explosion. At last Salosti decided to give up trying.

"Are you crazy?" Dani yelled panting. "You're supposed to beat Raiwox with me!"

"I'm not crazy," Salosti replied, "I wanna go home. It's not up to us anymore to save the Earth. Remember what Caispea said? There's no such thing as Destiny. So, now we can decide ourselves what we'll do. Somebody else can beat Raiwox. I don't care anymore."

"But, but…" Dani stammered. "But there's nobody else besides us. He said that Ferry and David are traitors. It's just you and me against the world. Even the citizens can't help, since most of them are either hiding or slaves now."

"Whatever! I should be dead anyway, but my heart and brain are still stuck in this freaking armor!"

Dani's persuasion was futile. He tried to explain how the victory would benefit both of them and the whole world.

"Look, if we don't do something and quick, the aliens and Raiwox will conquer this world, and you'll die anyway! If we find Caispea, we may find a way to stop your bomb. You'll survive, then you can go home and I'll return to Falgomduza. But in order to do all that I need your help."

Salosti still seemed apathetic.

"But even if we beat Raiwox, the whole world will be against me once they've seen Tainelm's video of me killing King Henrie. There's no way they could believe he was killing our allies whilst being controlled. Besides, we still have aliens in our back after beating Raiwox… Our opponents have planned everything ahead. Whatever happens, I will lose. It's like a ridiculously complex conspiracy…" Salosti started memorizing his home and friends and suddenly his mind changed. "… but I want to live in peace after all that I've gone through…"

"Do you mean you wanna die after everything is solved?" Dani asked aghast. Salosti nodded; he wanted to clear the vision of his soul by beating Raiwox; then start living his dream eternally in the heavens.

"Don't let the bomb kill you, Salosti! We're about to make this world a paradise and you're gonna leave? You were a holy terror when we first formed the army. I remember how you refused to accept me as I was. But over time you've changed into a perfect person. Just like this world: it was ruined, but now it's gonna be a paradise. Think about it, Salosti! Think, is that what you really want? Why'd you wanna die? Is it Liisa?"

"No," Salosti said quickly. *How does he know?* he thought. Then he continued: "… I mean yes, partially… but she's not the only reason. It's also that I must live without a soul in this armor… and it feels so empty!"

Dani touched his own breast and nodded. He had finally understood why his sense of humor had almost disappeared for the past few days: he felt empty too.

"I know what you mean," Dani said, "I don't want to live without a soul either… Could we die together with your bomb, since mine isn't working?"

"WHAT?"

"I feel just as terrible as you, living without a soul. Together we will save this world, and then leave for a place where we can be whole again, right?"

"Sure…"

"Okay, it's a promise! We'll meet the seventeenth day: the day our time runs out," Dani said smiling. Then he turned around to face the horizon. "I'm going to defeat Caispea and return King Henrie's body to his throne, alone. Meanwhile, you shall wait for me near the entrance to the Middle Island, okay?"

"Why can't I go with you?" Salosti asked, even though he knew the answer.

"Because the citizens don't trust you anymore after seeing Tainelm's video. They want your head on a plate, because in their eyes you are a traitor, even though it is actually the other way around. So, you'll need to be hiding from the people while you're waiting for me. I swear I'll come back before the 17th day so we have time to get Raiwox."

Dani turned around and walked away, leaving Salosti to the ruined laboratory. From the hole on the broken wall, Salosti saw a beautiful sunset. He stood alone for a long time, feeling happy for the first time in weeks. He knew that even though the common Destiny of mankind's happiness did not necessarily exist, his own was in Dani's hands.

The End of Chapter XI: Destiny

Chapter XII: Fight to the Death

Wuol and Valo had finally reached the cave on a green hill in Windmill Isles where they decided to live happily ever after. They did live happily, but they both felt that something was wrong. Valo and Wuol wanted that their old friend, Tainelm, would stop the madness and return to his old innocent self. Regardless of these worries, the two lived very safe life in their hiding place without being attacked by Kuoles or armored soldiers. One day, though, they wanted to finally stop the wars around the Earth. Valo and Wuol went to search for Tainelm and his underlings to knock some sense into their heads. This was the first step towards a better world.

Salosti was sitting on a tree beside a red-haired girl who wore blue and played a violin. Salosti looked at the clock of his lifetime and it showed that he had thirteen days and five hours left. He had received many letters from Ferry and David, but he had never even read them, because he knew the two were traitors. Caispea had leaked the last real Warriors some valuable information.

The lonely leader turned to face the girl on the blue.

"Hey, Aurora, do you think I should be waiting Dani, or is his promise to return only a subterfuge to waste my lifetime by making me wait forever? He could be another traitor."

The girl shrugged. "Don't ask me. You should know him."

"I know, he seems like a very good person to me, but I've been fooled by illusions for so many times that I can't be sure of anything ever again."

Aurora giggled. "You're right! Because even I am an illusion!"

As she said that, the rising sun melted her. She turned into water and streamed away leaving only her violin. It vanished as well afterwards.

Salosti wasn't surprised about the girl having been an illusion, but he was sad that he had to be alone again. He had seen countless illusions ever since the day he had departed from Dani's company. He was sure that Raiwox would use illusions against him in the final battle. He still sat on the tree, looking at the darkest castle he had ever seen: the Castle of Middle Island. Finally he saw a young man in the distance wearing a ragged armor and a sword. His greenish hair stuck from beneath his iron helmet. He was sloughing and hurt. He dragged himself to the tree ill at ease.

"He used illusions against me," he said panting, talking about Caispea. "Turned out that he became greedy and wanted to overthrow Raiwox so he could become the absolute ruler himself. But he didn't have what it takes to beat me." He turned a little more sympathetic as he smiled: "Ready for a one last fight?"

Salosti nodded even though he wasn't really ready. The two saw how the magical path opened to Middle Island now that even King Henrie's headless body had been returned to his throne by Dani.

The two Last Warriors took a small boat and sailed the way to the castle of eternal darkness. The invisible barriers were, indeed, gone.

Soon the two reached the shore. They started walking in the dark and misty island. They headed towards the castle that was only a few hundred meters away. The duo descended crystal stairs into a magical garden.

"So far so good," Salosti said, "But be careful for any kinds of traps..."

They entered the castle; the door was open. They walked through empty halls. There wasn't a single enemy anywhere.

"This is too easy! There's gotta be some kind of trick that'll kill us in a second!"

Salosti and Dani continued going onwards until they finally found the colossal throne room. And there he was: a black-haired, red eyed man leaning against his fist, sitting on his throne, bound to it with black chains. He was the lord and master, the root of all the evil in the universe.

"Raiwox!" Salosti whispered aloud, his voice echoing in the spacious throne room. The final tyrant's mere presence was so evil that agony of tears almost filled Salosti's eyes just by looking at his face. "I don't wanna do this," he thought. "But there's simply no way he's gonna come quietly with a talk. This fight is going to last until either of us will die."

Salosti nodded to Dani, and they summoned their swords and rushed towards Raiwox with great speed while casting strong spells on him. It was time to show all the skills they had learned so far. Raiwox didn't even move: the spells stopped in the mid-air in front of him. He slightly moved his hand and made the spells rebound on Salosti and Dani.

Then the tyrant snapped his fingers. Abruptly water masses rushed in the room and pulled the two under. Salosti swam to the surface and got on his feet on a platform above the water level, coughing. Suddenly sharp ice spikes rose from the ground and slashed his body. He recoiled and healed his wounds. He raised his head and guarded himself for the next attack. He looked around, but didn't see Dani or Raiwox. His body flinched as a thunder spell was cast on him from out of nowhere. He felt how invisible arms beat his body, and he fell to the water again. The water, though, evaporated because of heat that had invaded the room all of a sudden. Never had either of the Warriors faced someone with such strong magic and quick reflexes. His powers were truly inhuman.

Salosti found himself on the floor and got up immediately, already exhausted. Their opponent was too strong for them to win even with their best team work. Still there was no reason to give up since they had made it this far. Salosti decided that they would definitely win Raiwox so that all the sadness would finally go away. Dani was fighting Raiwox relentlessly. The last tyrant still hadn't moved from his golden throne as he only seemed to play around. But all of a sudden, he jumped off and ran towards Salosti, charging at him with his two spear-like swords. Salosti flinched. Raiwox made a complex combo of several attacks on Salosti. The hero was released from the series of attacks and found himself on the floor. He got up and observed his surroundings. He saw Raiwox charging at him from the side and dodged just in time. Raiwox had to take time to get back his balance from the missed attack. Salosti took the chance and cast a spell on him.

Raiwox grunted and levitated farther to recover. Salosti leapt high towards him, not allowing the respite, and landed a simple combo on him. The tyrant roared with anger and slashed Salosti with his swords. Salosti fell to the floor, landing smoothly by bending his knees. Just as he had landed, he raised his head upwards and saw Raiwox dashing against him from above, both of his swords sticking towards him.

Salosti made a shield that recoiled Raiwox. The Warrior removed the shield and counterattacked. His sword went right through Raiwox' belly which surprised him. It had been so easy to penetrate his defense. Salosti drew out his sword from his opponent's stomach, thinking he had ended it. Raiwox only laughed hollowly. Salosti was aghast.

"You fools! I'm immortal! Nobody can kill me!"

Raiwox flew back to his throne and seemed to have troubles in breathing. Salosti was confused and looked for Dani with his sight without results.

On a sudden, all the light in Salosti's sight disappeared along with the throne room. He fell on the ground and felt like he was fading away to a different world. All he could see now was himself surrounded by the infinite darkness.

"Where am I?"

He heard the reply in his mind: he knew that it was Raiwox who was using telepathy.

"You're inside my heart, Salosti," he spoke with an echoing double-voice. "A demon has taken over my body and controls me. He has controlled me all this time! The enticement won as he offered me the immortality. I craved for power and made a deal with him, agreeing to give him my body if he gave me infinite powers and the chance to live forever. I wanted these powers to be used for good, but he's the one controlling me now. The demon of greed uses my body to have absolute power, which is not what I wanted to happen. I can only hardly fight against him, so quickly, release me! I swear I won't hurt you or Dani if you just set me free from immortality. Quickly, before he takes over my mind again!"

Salosti heard the voice echoing in his mind until he found himself on the floor of the throne room again.

He saw Raiwox still sitting on his throne and Dani beside him.

"He talked to me telepathically, and told me that he won't kill us if we'll help him," Dani said.

"Me too! But is it a trap?" Salosti thought aloud.

"HURRY! IT"S NOT A TRAP! JUST GET RID OF MY "HEART BEARER"" Raiwox yelled like a madman so loudly that it startled both Warriors. Just then, a cage rose from the ground, somebody sitting there. Salosti and Dani ran towards the cage.

"Kill the person, whoever it is; it'll release me from immortality, and I promise I'll never cause any trouble again," Raiwox begged. Salosti now recognized who the one was sitting in the cage that now vanished, leaving the prisoner lying, chained on the floor.

"Liisa!" Salosti shouted.

"Vatarki!" Dani exclaimed.

The two looked at each other perplexed by each other's reactions.

"What're you talking…?" Salosti started, but Dani interrupted him.

"I think this is an illusion again! The Heart Bearer turns into the person who's the most important to the one who looks at it!"

"Illusion or not, I still don't wanna kill her."

"Me neither! Even if this is what it takes to kill the immortal, it is just too much to be asked!"

Raiwox was getting very angry.

"Do it! NOW! I could kill you! I could scatter your hearts and souls to million pieces. I could send the souls of your friends to hell! I could torture you to your death! I could make you watch your worst nightmares over and over again or realize them! I could do all that, BUT NO! I'm merciful! So, just do it!"

Dani and Salosti looked at each other and nodded.

"On three: One, two… three!"

Both stabbed their swords through the Heart Bearer. It screamed and Salosti and Dani, both felt a slash in their hearts. It was even more painful than either one of them had suspected. They closed their eyes, but heard the screams. Finally, when the shrieking had died away and the Heart Bearer vanished, the two opened their eyes to see if Raiwox had kept his word.

Raiwox stood straight, his eyes blinded, looking at nothingness. Salosti saw a black shadow rising from his body, screaming and fading away: at least the demon had died. But if they had made a deal, it meant that Raiwox, too should... Suddenly Raiwox couched and grabbed his stomach that started to fill with blood. He couched weakly one last time, and then fell to the floor dead; he had been released from eternal life.

The two Last Warriors were silent for a long time. Then Dani walked by Salosti and hugged him in tears of joy. "It's finally over!"

Salosti could feel the returning clarity of his vision in heaven; the spell of his soul's blindness had really been broken. He didn't know what to think: His dreams had finally come true. Peace was restored. So was freedom. And he would get to see his lost friends again and forget all the sadness.

"I know... it just... feels so unreal after all I've been through..." He managed to answer after a moment of silence.

Salosti and Dani walked outside the dark castle. It still was gloomy outside.

"I thought it'd be brighter after we beat him..." Dani said a little disappointed.

"So, what are we gonna do now?" Salosti asked.

"I'm going home with my brother," Dani replied. "I'll forgive him for what he's done now that everything is back to normal."

"What about our promise?" Salosti asked pointing at the bomb in his belly.

"Oh yeah, the bomb!" Dani said awkwardly. "You know, Salosti. I'm really afraid to die... I just wanna go home after this horrible adventure... I mean, it's been fun to get to know you and everyone else, but... you see what I mean... I just realized that the only thing I want is to go home with my bro... I know he did a lot of bad things, but inside he is good and I love him..."

"Yeah, I see," Salosti said angrily. "I'm going home as well. That's the only place I can return to now. Then, when it's my last day, I'll find a place where to die... alone!"

He turned around and marched towards his home, Dalik Islands. Dani felt bad for this kind of farewell from his best friend. He decided to find a way to save Salosti's life, even if it cost him his own.

End of Chapter XII: Fight to the Death

Chapter XIII: Legacy of Raiwox

Valo and Wuol found Tainelm with his underlings in a newly conquered town. Tainelm seemed sorrowful as walked by his friends.

"This conquering is depressing. I cannot enjoy the new land that's taken by force and violence. I tried to tell myself many times that our actions are justified, but I am tired of lying to myself. I'd rather be in our home, our sandbox, where everybody was happy and friends together; not any kinds of wars between the races or unfair share of power. Valo, Wuol, I wanna stop this madness and go with you to a place where everybody will live in harmony. I simply cannot justify killing in order to make my dreams come true."

Valo and Wuol were happy that Tainelm was back to normal.

"Well stop it! YOU are the only leader left now, since the Commander and General Caispea are gone," Valo said joyfully.

"That's what I'll do!" Tainelm said confidently and walked to his army to give orders of leaving planet Earth. The armored soldiers packed their camps and went on a journey to set all the slaves free from each town. After that Tainelm's troops left Earth and went to search for a new, empty planet that they could call home. Only thing that bothered Tainelm was that there was nothing he could do to the video he had shown the people. The Earthlings would never forgive Salosti for killing King Henrie. The propaganda and rumors had already made the hero a labeled villain.

The news about Raiwox' death reached the WOPlings. Tainelm and his friends were relieved. Now this planet was in peace, so they wouldn't feel bad for leaving it in an unsolved mess. The armored soldiers repaired places they had destroyed to make up for all the damage done. Medical aid was given to the injured, and the mayor who had provoked the war was not blamed for starting it all, because it was Raiwox who had manipulated his mind in the first place. Before the departure from the planet, Tainelm found Wuol and walked beside her. They admired the sunset together. The planet felt like it was reborn.

"Wuol... Will you marry me, once we find a new home?" Tainelm asked out of the blue.

A silence followed. Tainelm started fearing that she would give him a negative reply, but then she exclaimed:

"Oh, Tainelm I'd love to!"

The two kissed passionately. Valo looked from the side, proud of his friend, thinking "Well done, man!"

Soon almost all the WOPlings were sitting in their ship; everybody else except for Tainelm. Wuol was worried:

"What about Tainelm?" She asked, since the young man hadn't returned yet.

"He sent us a letter in which he promised to come afterwards," Valo said. "I wonder what business he has to do with that... uh, Salosti-kid."

"Salosti?" Wuol repeated. "Who the heck is Salosti?"

Salosti hadn't seen Kuoles or invaders for a long time. Also the Tax Ghosts had disappeared. The war seemed to be over as Raiwox had died. The sky was much brighter than ever before. The airships with their steam engines poisoning the air were gone. The people in the towns that Salosti went to weren't in chains anymore. The victorious leader still avoided the towns because of the video that had been shown to citizens. He was their enemy, no matter what he said he had done.

Our hero was resting by a lake near to the Dalik Islands. Sitting on a stone bridge, he took off his armor and threw it to the water, being sure that he had fought his final battle. He decided sleep to check if his vision in heaven had really become clear after defeating Raiwox.

He woke up in heaven with clarity in his sight. It had worked: now he was able to see everything as he had before. He spent his time by celebrating with everybody now that the Earth was saved from Raiwox. He also told his friends about the bomb that had only 12 days left to explode. It caused mixed emotions of grief and happiness in his friends; he would die in the real world, but on the other hand, he'd soon be in the heavens with them forever. Salosti spent ten hours in heaven. Then woke up and continued going onwards pointlessly.

After a while, Salosti had reached Dalik Islands. He knew the places from his memory. The towns were ruined after the battles. He walked through the empty streets until he saw a figure in the distance. The person noticed him and walked towards him. Salosti recognized the person when he was only three meters away

"Wow! You're back! I've heard terrible news about you! Is it true...?" Bill, Salosti's childhood friend, asked.

Salosti nodded. "Henrie was siding with the bad guys, because Raiwox had hypnotized him. I killed him, because he sabotaged our attempt to fix things, and nearly killed us."

Bill gasped. He, then, examined Salosti with his sight.

"You've changed: long and messy hair, black eyes, body full of scratches... Where the heck have you been?"

"I've been doing lots of stuff, like saving the world from Raiwox," Salosti said smiling. Bill didn't seem to believe him.

"Are you okay?" he asked. Salosti nodded starting to get annoyed by his friend's disbelief.

"Where's everybody? Alex, Willie, Jack, Alice…?" Salosti asked looking around while listing names of his childhood friends and acquaintances that lived in Dalik Islands.

"Things have changed while you were gone," Bill said. "Alex, like many others who wanted to escape reality, died for the drugs that she used. Alice's in a mental hospital after being mentally traumatized. Some escaped with their families. The rest are gone. Kuoles and aliens… Even I've changed…"

"But you're still you, aren't you?"

Bill shook his head.

"No, I'm not the same cheerful guy you knew back then. My parents died. I needed to kill others in order to survive… I am not the same Bill that once was your friend."

Salosti fell into depression. Had all of his effort been in vain? Returning home after saving the world was not worth it after all? He had lost all he had fought for in the first place.

Suddenly all the other citizens appeared out of nowhere and rushed towards them.

"There he is! Get him!"

Salosti tried to calm down the crowd in vain. "Take it easy, people! I just set you free from Raiwox and aliens. Everything's okay now, so why can't we all be happy now?"

"Because you killed our beloved king, that's why! And you're only trying to lie to us! Nobody like you could ever beat Raiwox!" someone from the crowd yelled.

"That's right!" another one agreed, "Aren't you that infamous delinquent who escaped from your home? A wretched child like you is only capable of causing us good people harm."

"What're you standing for? Get him!" the leader of the crowd yelled. The people drew out some weapons and wailed a vindictive warcry. Salosti had no choice but to run. He could have handled the people with his sword and magic easily, but he didn't want to hurt civilians, despite the fact that they had not changed at all; still all prejudicial and mean towards him because of his background. Our hero headed outside the town and outran his chasers.

Salosti stopped by the same bridge on which he had rested the last night. He panted for a moment until he caught his breath again. He was all sweaty, and thoughts were running in his mind once again. He wondered why Bill had changed so much, and why Alex had started doing drugs. It didn't match the view of them that Salosti had always had.

"Is it because of passing time why everything had changed, or was it because I had been gone...?" he thought aloud. It felt so wrong that he couldn't go home after his long and painful journey. He sighed and lay down. "I'm broke! Maybe I should hit the hay".

Salosti woke up, somebody shaking him. He wiped his eyes yawning. It was Dani. The Falgomduzian seemed happier than ever.

"Good news, Salosti!" He said smiling widely. Salosti was anticipating a way to stop his bomb from Dani (even though he didn't want it).

"I just got a letter of inheritance. Turns out that I'm a far relative of Raiwox! It means that I'm gonna be the heir to the throne in the Middle Island!"

Salosti wasn't excited.

"Don't accept the honor! We don't need a fourth king, we never have! It's gonna cause only more wars and chaos! Besides, weren't you supposed to return home?"

Dani's smile froze in his face. He stuttered "But... but I'm not gonna be like HIM! I'm gonna be a good king. One who loves his people like Henrie!"

Salosti shook his head and grabbed Dani from his shirt.

"Stop being crazy! Pull yourself together! Just when we are finished with the madness you're gonna start it over!"

Dani released himself from Salosti's grip.

"Get off! I'm a noble person. You're not even allowed to talk to me! If you're not happy you can stay home while I go to my throne in Middle Is..."

"I won't let you!" Salosti withdrew his sword and slashed Dani's arm with it out of aggression. Dani flinched and stepped back in rage. His eyes were blinking with madness.

"Okay, if it's fight you're seeking for... I'll race you to the throne! If I touch it, I'll become the king legally. If you get there first, I'll listen to you... NOT!"

He pushed Salosti and started running. Salosti started chasing him.

Why, Dani? He thought. *Why won't you just go home to your family and let me forget this awful sadness? What happened to you? Why does everyone change so drastically?*

The race was relentless by both Salosti and Dani; neither one wanted to give up. Dani was sure that he could find a way to possess an eternal life once he'd become the king. His fear of death controlled his mind. Salosti was desperate when thinking about having to start all over. He had sacrificed so much, even though he shouldn't have had to, without giving up, even after he had heard the truth about Destiny and Orders. He had done so much without gaining his reward. His home was ruined and friends manipulated, and they'd never know the truth about his long journey.

Dani ran faster than Salosti (even though their athletic skills were at the same level), because Salosti hadn't rested enough for a long time. The chase all the way to Middle Island was very arduous. Salosti felt bad when thinking that he'd have to fight against Dani. He knew that the Heir of the Cursed King was a good person inside just like his brother, but he also knew that hatred between old friends was the grimmest hatred of them all.

Finally the two reached the dark castle of Middle Island. Both hurried in, all the way to the throne room where the empty throne stood mighty. Dani hurried to touch it and felt the power of it streaming inside of him. He laughed maniacally, then turned around and raised his arm. A powerful spell shackled Salosti with dark chains. A cage rose around him and he felt how something warm glowed inside him. Dani had made Salosti his Heart Bearer.

"You're accused of being against the will of mine! I, the new king and ruler of Middle Island, sentence you to be my Heart Bearer until the end of time." He clapped his hands and shadowy figures, his underlings, appeared.

"Take him to the highest tower! Then I can always see him!" He ordered, and the shadow-minions lifted the cage and took it away, leaving Dani alone in the room. He cut his own arm violently with a dagger and saw that it didn't bleed. He laughed insanely, mad out of the almighty power he possessed; he had been spared of his worst fear, death. He was finally immortal.

Dani had been as the king of Earth for three days. The whole world was aware of him being the new ruler. He had created high taxes and mighty armies. His power was indestructible. He had some worries regardless of his powers, though: his armies sometimes killed innocent people against his orders, some citizens were planning revolutions against him, and worst of all, he saw Salosti everyday in the tower sorrowful. Sometimes he even cried a bit. He decided to set Salosti free from the duty of Heart Bearer. The former leader of the Warriors was his best friend after all.

Dani set his prisoner free. He sentenced Salosti to exile instead, hiding what he really wanted. The warrior disappeared and nobody heard about him for a long time. Dani thought that he'd be relieved from guilt after that, but he was wrong. The sorrows continued and he wasn't in control of anything anymore. Even though he tried to, he couldn't set the people free from his unfair rules. It was as if somebody else was controlling him…

Salosti walked the quiet, empty streets of an unknown, dark town. It was raining hard and only the flashlights of the shops and inns around lit the darkness. Salosti didn't want to sleep, and he hadn't slept for many days, because he wanted to enjoy his final days on Earth. For some reason he wasn't excited anymore about getting to see his dead friends in heaven.

"Why can't I ever be pleased?" He thought. He was very tired, but he couldn't go to an inn or make a camp, since he was on the wanted list; wherever he went, people seeing him tried to catch him. He was a lunatic murderer in the eyes of the world; the assassin who callously murdered the beloved King Henrie. He had heard those lies so many times that he almost started to believe in them by himself.

The heavy rain lashed Salosti's face, but he felt hardly anything now that he was a robot. Some dark creatures that the lone young man had fought in the past appeared. Salosti allowed them to try to hurt him. "Come on! Is that all you got?"

The shapeless creatures clawed, bit, and hit him with objects, but he only laughed so that his black eyes grew wide. He drew out his sword and hit the ground with it while casting a deadly spell that he had never used before. All the twenty enemies around him died at once. His mind was bewitched with the passion of a madman. His nebulous memories came to his mind: the deaths of Liisa's brother, Eric, The King of Snow Town, Akii's army controlled by two traitorous men whose hands he had trusted those lives to … Salosti had denied that he had anything to do with all thpse deaths. He had never told anyone, and it felt terrible to keep it all inside. All he had was himself. Everything else was illusion to him. He couldn't trust anybody. He no longer had any friends. He was losing everything, including his sanity.

Salosti found himself lying on the street, rain still dripping on his soaked clothes. He thought that what he had just done had been a dream. "Was it a dream, or am I really going insane?" He was horrified about the way he had acted against his will. If this continued, he would probably end up killing normal humans too. He glanced at the time of his bomb. 2- 13:34, it showed.

"So, I still have two more days to live," he thought and raised his head seeing the dark castle of Middle Island in the distance. Aurora over the edifice made the other side of the castle shine bright, lifting the shadows off. Salosti knew now what he had to do.

The dream continues. Is there no end? Please end my pain. Give me the power to wake up. I beg you. Bestow on me your forgiveness.

The tower had become dilapidated over time. No one noticed it anymore as anything else than a mere ruin. And no one would have guessed that there still was someone inside...

Dani felt how the shadows pulled his body back and forced him to lie on his throne. He wasn't able to move and he was mad at himself.

"Why the heck was I so greedy, even as my best friend warned me? Why wouldn't I just listen to him just this once?" He put down his head and started to sleep to escape his kingdom of shadows and enter the heavenly joy.

Dani woke up quickly as somebody entered the throne room. He tried to rise up, but failed. He yelled at the unseen figure.

"Who goes there?"

Salosti appeared from behind the door. "It's me".

"Salosti, I just wanted to see you! What are you doing here?"

The exiled hero pointed at the bomb that showed that he had only seventeen hours left.

 "We had a promise, remember?" He said. Dani scratched his head sadly.

"I've heard terrible news about you, Salosti. They call you a killer. Is that true? Have you really reached the mental breakdown?"

Salosti shook his head. "I don't know! I'm not sure if I really have lost my mind. I might have. But the only thing that I remember for sure was our promise."

Dani got up, breaking the shadowy chains.

"I want to be free again!" He cried so loud that Salosti was frightened. Dani continued "I don't deserve this; you should have had the immortality since my bomb didn't even work! And I did not think what would happen to my brother or my family. I couldn't control myself; I think it's this throne! It must be cursed. That's why Raiwox was cursed too, and taken over by a demon! The same must have happened to me! I could feel my thought process getting blurry ever since we defeated Raiwox. I must've inherited the curse."

Salosti nodded. He understood perfectly. They might both have been insane right then- Salosti because of his isolation and all the lies about him, and Dani because of the demon-, but at least they understood each other.

Dani summoned the cage in which the Heart Bearer sat, shaking and crying.

"I'll take him," Dani said. "Because this all is my fault."

Salosti stepped to hold him back.

"NO! I'll take HER, because I'm a killer naturally. I've cost the lives of more people than necessary. My whole army was terminated because I was a bad leader and I couldn't even admit it." He withdrew his sword and looked at the shapeless Heart Bearer that transformed into Liisa, looking directly into his eyes. Salosti stood still and the Heart Bearer transformed again. It kept on transforming to all the people he knew: Hajosiko, Kaste, Aurora, Bill, Alice, Ferry, David, Lumi, Tainelm, Vatarki, Eric, The three tyrant kings, Raiwox, Wanhaz, Henrie, Akii and finally back to Dani.

Salosti knew why the Heart Bearer had transformed so many times to different persons: the most important thing that he possessed now was his memories. Now he remembered his journey from beginning to this moment. He remembered all the treasured adventures and sentimental moments that he had experienced during the journey, and which he had stored inside. He had learned about friendship, love, and teamwork... For the first time in his life Salosti was actually happy that Akii had chosen him. He finally remembered who he really was inside.

Salosti faced the Heart Bearer that was now only a shapeless creature.

"I don't kill you, because I want to take your life, but because my friend needs me," he said and charged at the Heart Bearer. After being impaled t fell to the floor and faded away.

Dani started couching. "Destroy the throne, so that nobody ever takes over this world again," he said. "The demon must be inside it." Salosti destroyed the throne with ease. He glanced at the timer and hurried beside Dani.

"Hang on, buddy! Only seven minutes left," he said and healed Dani's wounds.

"But now nobody will ever know the truth about what happened to me, and who really defeated Raiwox," Dani said sadly.

"WRONG!" Somebody shouted from the entrance. It was Tainelm.

"I'll tell the others the truth about you!" He said, "I'll tell your honorable legend on and on and make sure that nobody ever forgets it! I came only to apologize and say goodbye forever, but after seeing all this, I must say that nobody in this universe shall forget your story; the story of true, eternal friendship. You two didn't only face your fears, but you also carried on, even as you saw your friends fall one by one. And the most honorable thing is that you two willingly gave your lives for this world to have a second chance to live in harmony. You will be remembered as heroes who defeated Raiwox and brought back the peace."

"Thanks, Tainelm!" Both Dani and Salosti said.

Salosti smiled. "Two more minutes," he said. "Just a sec."

Salosti closed his eyes and flowed away from his body.

He was in heaven, once more. He found Liisa and walked by her.

"It is almost time... Soon I'll be here with you... forever!"

"I know. I'm so happy yet so sad," said Liisa and kissed Salosti. The leader told all the others that soon he'd be there to stay. Wanhaz's soul walked beside him.

"You've done well, son. I'm proud of you."

Salosti said. "I've got to go now! See y'all in a minute!"

He flowed back into his body.

The throne room returned to our hero's vision. He knew that the time was drawing near, but there were still some things he was concerned about.

"Tainelm, what are you going do after this?" Dani asked, as if having read his friend's mind.

"I'm going live with my new wife, Wuol, and my friends in a new world. They got a head start, so it may be hard to find them, but I'll make it."

"Tainelm, if you happen to see my brother, Vatarki, please tell him to go home without me," Dani said.

"You can count on that," Tainelm said.

"And, Tainelm!" Salosti said. "Tell Wuol that Wanhaz is in good condition in the heavens with me and my army!"

Tainelm nodded.

Salosti looked at the timer. It was the last minute. He told Tainelm to go far away for the explosion. Then he grabbed Dani's hand and shook it.

"Goodbye, friend" he said. "It was an honor to know you."

"Likewise," Dani replied.

One last time Salosti looked at his friend, one last tear dropping down his cheek.

Then it happened: A volcanic explosion, an insanely loud boom, and an enormous quake. The structures of the dark castle collapsed and the two heard Tainelm cry their names. Salosti felt how his body disintegrated, and he felt something very sweet in his spirit.

At last he had left his prison, like Tainelm who had gone home. He had left the spiritless body. He knew that Tainelm would live happily, now since the war was over and he'd go to Valo and Wuol, searching for a new home. He knew that, thanks to Tainelm, he and Dani would be dying as heroes, not traitors. He knew that the Earth was now safe and sound like it had been the day it was created. And he was happier than ever before; he knew he was finally free.

The End

Printed by Books on Demand GmbH, Norderstedt / Germany